Killer

Maple

Cookies

Book Three

in

Killer Cookie

Cozy Mysteries

By

Patti Benning

Copyright 2016 Summer Prescott Books

Author's Note: On the next page, you'll find out how to access all of my books easily, as well as locate books by best-selling author, Summer Prescott. I'd love to hear your thoughts on my books, the storylines, and anything else that you'd like to comment on – reader feedback is very important to me. Please see the following page for my publisher's contact information. If you'd like to be on her list of "folks to contact" with updates, release and sales notifications, etc…just shoot her an email and let her know. Thanks for reading!

Also…

…if you're looking for more great reads, from me and Summer, check out the Summer Prescott Publishing Book Catalog:

http://summerprescottbooks.com/book-catalog/ for some truly delicious stories.

Contact Info for Summer Prescott Publishing:

Twitter: @summerprescott1

Blog and Book Catalog: http://summerprescottbooks.com

Email: summer.prescott.cozies@gmail.com

And…look up The Summer Prescott Fan Page on Facebook – let's be friends!

If you're an author and are interested in publishing with Summer Prescott Books – please send Summer an email and she'll send you submission guidelines.

TABLE OF CONTENTS

KILLER MAPLE
COOKIES

Book Three in Killer Cookie Cozy Mysteries

CHAPTER ONE

"Are you sure you fixed everything? It's not going to break down on me halfway home?" Lilah Fallon asked the hunched elderly man standing next to her. They were assessing the little powder-blue, beat-up hunk of metal that was her car.

"It's as good as new," he said, patting the hood, which popped open. He quickly shut it, then tested it again. It stayed shut. "Well, maybe I shouldn't say that, but it's in better shape than it was when you dropped it off. It runs now, and that's the important thing, eh?"

"As long as it will get me around town, I'm happy with it," Lilah told him. She couldn't wait to have her own vehicle again. She'd spent the last couple of months walking everywhere, or borrowing her neighbor's when she needed it. "How much do I owe you?"

He told her the number and she winced. That would be almost all of her savings from her temporary job at a local farm over the Halloween season. Still, she needed her car back. With a sigh, she reached into her purse and pulled out her checkbook. The little auto shop didn't accept credit cards, so she would have to pay for this the old-fashioned way.

A few minutes later and a thousand dollars poorer, she pulled out of the auto shop's parking lot and turned right, toward home. Having her car back gave her a wonderful feeling of freedom. No more borrowing Margie's car, and no more walking everywhere under the sun. This would make it so much easier for her to achieve her next goal: finding the perfect place to open her cookie shop.

Lilah turned into her driveway and parked the car in front of her little yellow house. She listened to the sound of the vehicle idling for a moment, hardly able to believe how good it sounded. With a smile, she turned the key and let the old car rattle into silence before she got out and headed up to her front porch.

The yellow house was a rental, but she loved it as if it were her own. It had been her home for over two years, and she could hardly imagine living anywhere else. Her front yard was large and grassy, and the porch had a set of comfortable outdoor chairs and a small table where she liked to drink her morning coffee. The back yard opened up to a tangle of undergrowth, making her feel like she was in the middle of a jungle, especially when it was raining. To her left was an empty plot overgrown with trees and bushes, and to her right lived her friend and mentor, Margie Hatch.

Margie had strongly encouraged Lilah to think about opening her own cookie shop. The older woman was a prolific baker, and had taken Lilah under her wing just a few short months ago. Lilah had discovered a skill and passion for baking that surprised her. She'd never taken much time to cook before, having preferred the premade, easy-to-heat-up meals that she had largely grown up on, but now she was completely hooked. There was something intensely rewarding about taking a pile of ingredients and like magic, creating a plate full of delicious cookies.

A bubble of happiness rose inside her as she unlocked her front door. She was so excited to get started on the next step of her journey. She had told everyone who would listen about her plan to open a cookie shop in town; surprisingly, her friends all seemed to think it was a good idea. Given her track record with new jobs, she had thought that they would have more doubts. It made her glad to think that they had such faith in her.

"Hey, Winnie," she said as she opened her door to reveal her beagle waiting eagerly on the other side. She wasn't wagging her tail as much as her entire body. "I was only gone for about half an hour."

Oscar, her orange tabby cat, gave her a sleepy look from his spot in the sun on the windowsill. He probably hadn't even noticed that she was gone. She walked over to stroke him before heading into the kitchen with Winnie at her heels to deposit her purse and car keys on the table.

"Here's a cookie," she said to the dog. "A dog cookie, not a human one, though I know you like those too."

The treat vanished from her hand as if the beagle was part vacuum cleaner. Doing her best to ignore Winnie's hopeful stare for more, Lilah pulled a pitcher of filtered water out of the fridge and poured herself a glass, glancing at the stove's clock as she took a sip. She had twenty minutes to shower, dry her hair, and get over to Margie's. She would need to hurry if she didn't want to keep the woman—her friend, business partner, and neighbor all rolled into one—waiting.

Fifteen minutes later, refreshed from her short shower, Lilah headed out her front door and across the yard to Margie's house. She was unsurprised to see a car that she recognized next to her friend's; it looked like Reid Townsend was over at Margie's house again.

Reid had grown up next door to Margie—in the very house that Lilah now rented, in fact—and the older woman seemed to view him as a sort of son. She often had him come over to help out with tasks around the house such as fixing her screen door, replacing a broken porch step, or just helping out with yard work. Reid didn't seem to mind, and somehow he always seemed to be over there when Lilah was going to go over.

Today, it looked like he was scrubbing the siding. He was up on a tall ladder with a push broom and a hose. As Lilah walked by, he looked down and the ladder wobbled threateningly. Alarmed, she reached out to steady it.

"Hey, Lilah," he called down, looking unconcerned. "How are you doing? I see you got your car back." He nodded toward the blue vehicle in her driveway.

"Yeah, it took a while, but she's in working order again." Cautiously, she let go of the ladder. "I've got to go in and talk to Margie. Are you going to be okay out here on your own? Shouldn't you have someone... I don't know, spotting you or something?"

"Are you worried about me?" He flashed her a grin.

"I just know how badly she'd feel if you fell or broke something because of the work you were doing for her."

"Oh." He looked slightly disappointed. "Well, I'll be careful. It's steadier than it looks."

She was about to knock on the screen door of her friend's house when he spoke again.

"Hold on, I almost forgot. Are you still planning on opening that shop and selling cookies?"

"I am," she said, looking up at him again. "And yes, I'll have all of the cookies you need done in time for the Thanksgiving event at your work."

Reid was her very first official customer. Shortly after he heard about her plan to start her own business, he jumped at the chance to place a large order with her. She wasn't set up for baking on that scale yet, but still, she was hardly complaining. He had paid handsomely, and had even offered to hand out her business cards at the event. The fact that she didn't have business cards yet hadn't deterred her from jumping on the opportunity.

"I'm not doubting you. I was just going to say, if you haven't found a store front yet, I know someone who's thinking of selling his building. It's zoned for retail, and I think he'll agree to a reasonable price. If you're interested, I could take you to see it this week."

"Really?" Lilah asked, her interest piqued despite her long-standing resolution not to encourage Reid's unrequited attraction to her. "I haven't found anything yet. I'd love to see it."

"How about Tuesday?" he asked with a smile. This time she returned it.

"Sure."

Inside, Margie greeted her with a smile. The older woman's arms were full of bags of flour and sugar. She seemed to be clearing out her rather extensive pantry.

"What's going on?" Lilah asked, breathing in the familiar, warm vanilla scent of her friend's kitchen.

"I'm making a basket for you to take home with you," she said. "You're going to need a lot of flour for all of those cookies you're making for Reid."

"What are you talking about?" Lilah asked. "I thought we were baking them here."

"Oh, you didn't get my message? My son and his family are coming a week early. Something about extra vacation time his boss wants him to use up. I won't be able to help as much as I'd thought. I hope you understand, Lilah, I wouldn't want to disappoint you like this if I could help it. It's just that I see them so rarely."

"Don't worry, I'm sure I'll be able to handle it on my own," Lilah said as she took a bag of flour from her friend, trying to ignore her alarm at the thought of having to make hundreds of cookies on her own. "You just enjoy seeing your family."

"Thank you, dear. If you can make it, I'd love for you to come to dinner the night after they arrive. I've told them all about you and your dreams, and I'm sure they're dying to meet you."

"If you're sure I wouldn't be intruding…"

"You're family too," Margie said firmly. "I don't want you to ever feel like you're not welcome here, whether my family's here or not."

Touched beyond words, Lilah helped her friend load up the large wicker basket of cookie ingredients in silence. Her life might not be perfect, but she certainly had been blessed with some exceptional friends.

CHAPTER TWO

D espite her friend's kind words, Lilah couldn't help but feel like something of an intruder as she walked toward her neighbor's house a couple of evenings later. She had watched Margie's family arrive from her living room window the night before. The man and woman, her friend's son and daughter-in-law, had unloaded a surprising amount of luggage from their minivan, making her think that either they had overpacked, or they were planning on staying a while. Their three children had seemed happy and well behaved, each of them giving their grandmother a hug before hurrying inside.

Lilah, an only child whose business-traveling father had been absent more often than not, never felt exactly comfortable at big family events. Never having had younger siblings, she hadn't had much practice talking to little kids, and the thought of three of them at once made her anxious. These were Margie's grandchildren, after all. What if she said the wrong thing, and made everyone at the table hate her?

Telling herself to calm down, she raised her fist to knock on the door. It opened before she made contact, and she found herself looking down at a young boy. He looked up at her questioningly, but didn't say anything.

"Um, hi," she said. "I'm Lilah. Mar— your grandmother invited me to dinner."

He pushed the screen door open, which she took as an invitation to come in, then ran away with a giggle. Already feeling somewhat off balance, Lilah let herself into the house. She was relieved to see Margie come into the kitchen just as she shut the door behind her.

"There you are, Lilah, I was just about to send Alexandria over to get you."

"I told you, Gran, I want people to call me Lexi now," said a voice from behind the older woman. A tween girl poked her head around her grandmother to take a good look at Lilah. "Mom wanted me to ask you where the knives are. We need one more to finish setting the table."

"They're in that drawer over there, sweetie," Margie said. "No, the one next to the dishwasher. There you go." She turned back to Lilah. "That's my granddaughter, Alexandria. The little boy you met is Jacob, and the other little girl is Annie."

"They're cute," Lilah said, not at all sure if it was the right thing to say. "I'm glad that they're getting the chance to come and visit you."

"Me too. I don't get to see them nearly enough. I think I might take a trip to go see them next year. The little ones are growing so quickly."

A timer went off, and Margie hurried over to the oven. Cracking it open, she grabbed a meat thermometer from the counter and stuck it into a delicious-looking ham.

"It's ready," she said after a moment. "Lilah, dear, will you take the fruit salad out of the fridge? I'm going to go tell everyone that it's time to eat."

By the time the four adults and three children had gotten themselves seated around the table, Lilah was convinced that Margie's family had been snatched right out of a fairy tale. The children were polite, her son and daughter-in-law scrambled to make sure that Margie did as little work as possible, and the food, of course, looked like it belonged on the front cover of a magazine.

The table practically groaned under the weight of ham, green bean casserole, mashed potatoes, rolls, and fruit salad. If this was what a casual family dinner looked like for Margie's family, then Lilah couldn't wait to see what her friend whipped up on Thanksgiving. Her stomach growled embarrassingly loudly as she unfolded her napkin and put it on her lap.

"Now that everyone's seated at last," Margie said, "I'd like to take a moment to introduce everyone to my dear friend and neighbor, Lilah. She's been a wonderful help these last couple of years. Lilah, this is my son Robby, and his wife Eliza."

There was a round of the obligatory "nice to meet you" and "I've heard so much about you" while the children began serving themselves food, and in no time at all the daughter-in-law, Eliza, had drawn Lilah into a conversation about work.

"Margie tells me you work at the diner part time," Eliza said, pausing to take a roll from the basket that was being passed around. "Is that all you do?"

"I've had other jobs here and there," Lilah told her. "In fact, I just got done with a seasonal job at a local farm."

"A bright woman like you, I thought you were bound to be on some sort of career path," Eliza said. She cut a small piece off of her slice of ham. "Oh well, it just goes to show how valuable a good education is, especially in this economy."

"I have a bachelor's degree," Lilah said icily. "I just haven't found the right career yet. And I'm perfectly happy working at the diner."

Margie turned toward them, smiling, as she passed along the green bean casserole. She didn't seem to notice the frigid atmosphere between the two women. "How is everything?" she asked.

"Wonderful," Lilah said, quickly arranging a smile on her face for her friend. "The potatoes are just perfect. I can't wait to try the beans."

"Lilah was just telling me about all of the jobs that she's had," Eliza said.

"Oh, has she mentioned the cookie store?" Margie asked.

"No, she hasn't. Is that another one of the places she's worked at?"

"Oh, no, no. She's planning on opening a cookie shop in town. She's very gifted at baking. I think it's a phenomenal idea."

"That sounds nice," Eliza said, turning back toward Lilah. "Expensive, though, I'd imagine."

"I'm her investor," Margie told her daughter-in-law with an even bigger smile. "I can't wait to see the cookie store come to life."

Eliza shot a glance toward her husband, but he was busy trying to convince their youngest child, Annie, that the green beans weren't going to poison her. Her expression annoyed, she turned back to Margie.

"Do you think that's really a good idea, Marge? What are you going to do if the business fails? I hope you've spoken to an attorney about this. You should draw something up in case she decides to run away with the money."

"I would never do that," Lilah gasped. "Margie's my friend. I didn't even ask her for the money, she offered."

"Now, Eliza, I know you're just speaking out of concern for me, but I think that was going a little too far. I trust Lilah completely. Even if she *had* come to me and asked for the money, I would have been happy to give it. As it is, I was the one that offered it to her because I believe that she's going to make a marvelous baker, and I know that she would do the same for me if our positions were reversed."

Lilah was touched. She hadn't realized what a good friend Margie was until recently, but now she was firmly convinced that she had gotten very lucky that day she had decided to move into the yellow house.

"What's going on over here?" Robby asked, turning around to face his wife. He seemed to have succeeded in convincing his daughter to eat the beans; she was making slow but steady headway through the small pile on her plate. "Are you ladies arguing?"

"No, I was just concerned about your mother, that's all," Eliza said. "Did you know she's going into business with Lilah here?"

"I think she might have mentioned something about that over the phone." He shifted his attention to Margie and Lilah. "Congratulations, you two. You're opening some sort of bakery, right? Have you thought of any names?"

"We're going to sell cookies, mainly," Lilah told him. "And I've been completely stumped when it comes to names. It should be something original and cute but easy for the customers to remember. Do you have any ideas?"

"I don't know," he mused. "The Cute Cookie? The Cookie Emporium? Carefree Cookies?"

"Those are all pretty good ideas," Lilah said.

"Cookies 'R' Us?" Lexi suggested. "Or Gram's Gooey Cookies?"

"Does the name have to have the word 'cookie' in it?" Eliza asked. "Chocolate Creations, Margie's Bakery, Bite-Sized Baked

Goods…" She trailed off with a sniff. "Though I suppose you have more important things to be thinking of than names if you're going to go through with this."

"I think it's a fun idea," Robby said. "Who doesn't like cookies? If Ma says you're good, I trust her judgment."

Lilah gave him a quick smile of thanks, and the conversation turned to the children's classes and grades. She was glad that the topic had moved away from the cookie shop; Eliza had unknowingly touched upon a subject that she was already concerned about. Was she taking advantage of Margie's friendship and good heart by accepting her loan to help start up the cookie shop?

PATTI BENNING

CHAPTER THREE

Despite the fact that Lilah usually avoided seeing Reid when she could—she had determined long ago that the business world and all those associated with it just weren't good for her—she was practically bubbling over with excitement for their meeting that Tuesday to look at the building that Reid's acquaintance was selling. She knew that the chances of her finding the right store front for the cookie shop the first time she went out to look at a place were slim, but it still felt like a monumental step. The cautious part of her warned that it might be smarter to find a place to lease until the cookie shop got on its feet, but she'd never been very good about listening to her cautious side. She was the type of person that went all in when she made up her mind, and this was no exception.

Reid pulled into her driveway early Tuesday afternoon, in spite of her insistence that she would be perfectly happy to meet him at the store. She had just finished her morning shift at the diner, and her hair was still wet from her hurried shower—there were a lot of things that she liked about working at the diner, but the clinging onion-and-fried-meat smell was not one of them—when he knocked at her door. She let him in and left him in the kitchen to be entertained by Winnie, who was more than happy to accept the responsibility, while she finished getting ready.

"Okay," she said when she re-emerged a few minutes later with her hair partially dried and pulled back into a messy bun. "Where exactly is this store?"

"Right along Main Street," he told her. "I'm sure you've passed it a hundred times. I think it would be the perfect place for a cookie shop."

Lilah couldn't help but agree with him on that. Vista wasn't a big town, and nearly every noteworthy store was situated along Main Street. It was prime real estate property for any retail shop or restaurant. The little Alabama town was set along a highway that went down to the coast, so shops along the center street saw not only local shoppers, but a large amount of tourist traffic as well.

Reid's car was black, sleek, and expensive looking, and couldn't have been more different than her beat-up blue rust bucket. She felt self-conscious about her slightly damp hair, and made an effort to sit up straight so it didn't touch his leather seats. The interior of his car smelled new, and she wondered fleetingly how much it had cost him. Even she could admit sometimes that there was something to be said for a nice, comfortable corporate job at a successful business.

"Do you want to stop anywhere on the way?" he asked her as he started up the engine, which was so quiet that she could hardly hear it.

"No, not unless you wanted to stop somewhere," she said. "I'm just excited to see the store."

"All right, straight there," he promised. He put the car into gear and pulled out of the driveway, turning right, toward town, and giving the car a generous amount of gas as they sped off.

Lilah fell in love with the store the instant that she saw it. It was nestled between a dry cleaner's and a small used book shop. Directly across the street was a gym, which she found a bit ironic, and it just made her love the place all the more. In its current incarnation, the store was a sandwich shop. A handwritten sign reading *Permanently Closed* hung in the window, though the lights were on and she could see people inside.

"Reid, it's perfect," she said as he effortlessly parallel parked on the opposite side of the road.

"You haven't even gone in yet," he said, but he was smiling.

They got out of the car and walked across the road, Lilah's eyes taking in every aspect of the building while trying to imagine it done up with the cookie shop's name and colors. She reached for the door, which currently read Talbot's Sandwiches, but it opened before she could touch it. A burly man with messy, greying brown hair strode out, knocking her back.

"Sorry," she said, as Reid steadied her stumble. The man ignored her. He turned to look back inside the store, and his bloodshot eyes narrowed to a glare.

"I know where you live, Talbot," he said. "And I'm not going to rest until I get what's coming to me."

"Oh, go home, Andrew. You're drunk. Come back when you actually know what you're saying, and maybe we can make a deal," said a voice from inside.

Andrew made a rude hand gesture, then stormed off down the sidewalk. Timidly, Lilah reached for the door again. Again, it opened without her touching it. This time the man behind it looked much friendlier, even if he did have bags under his eyes and a stain on his shirt.

"Sorry about that," he said to her and Reid. "That was an old friend of mine who drinks too much. I asked him not to come around anymore, but I doubt he remembers. Are you the two that wanted to take a look at the building?"

Lilah nodded. "That would be me. I'm Lilah Fallon."

"Pete Talbot." He shook her hand, then gestured her inside. "It's not huge, but it's in pretty good shape. What business are you in?"

"I'd be opening a cookie shop," she told him. Reid was hanging back and letting her do most of the talking, for which she was grateful.

"Well, this place would be perfect for that," Pete said. "There's a full set up in back, and I've got a glass display refrigerator that I'd be happy to sell with the place if you think it'd be useful. As a matter of fact, pretty much anything you see here can be sold along with the store. The cash register, refrigerated glass counter, the racks in the back… I use them for bread, but you could use them for cookies. I don't need any of this stuff anymore."

Her happiness as she looked around the store was tempered by the knowledge that the only reason that all of this was available was due to the fact that Pete's dream had failed. She felt terrible for him, and also scared for herself. If he hadn't been able to succeed, then what made her think that she would be able to?

Still, she adored the little shop. It was small, but perfect. The fact he was also selling a lot of the equipment that she would need was a huge bonus in her eyes. Sure, some of it was older equipment, but if he was willing to sell all of it at a good price, not having to go out and buy new appliances would save her hundreds or even thousands of dollars. Just like Reid had said, it was the perfect location for a cookie shop. It was walking distance from pretty much anywhere in town, and it had a wonderful display window out front to catch the eyes of pedestrians. The front room was cozy, with room for a display, the register and counter, and just enough room leftover for her to put a little table and chairs without making it feel crowded.

The kitchen was a bit bigger, with ample counter space on which she could roll out cookie dough, and two large, stainless-steel sinks. There was a small bathroom as well, and a room that could be used as a storage area or in a pinch, an office. The second door opened out back to the parking lot that the shop shared with two other nearby businesses.

"What do you think?" Pete asked her when he was done with the tour. "I know it's not huge, but it might work out okay for a new business…"

"It's perfect," Lilah said firmly. "Thank you so much for taking the time to show it to me." She hesitated, not sure what the next step would be. Should she show it to Margie first? The older woman *was* her investor, and she deserved a say in what happened with the money.

"I'll give you a few days to think it over and talk to whoever's going into this with you before you make a decision," he told her. "My sister keeps bugging me about this place—I've got a meeting with her tomorrow, in fact—but I've already made up my mind that I'm not going to put it on the market until next week, so you should have a little bit of time to mull it over without worrying about someone snatching it out from under you. Here's my asking price..." he scribbled it down on a napkin and handed it to her. "But I'm willing to negotiate. My main goal is to get it sold, and fast. I've, ah, run into some financial issues of late that I need to solve as soon as possible." He looked embarrassed. "Anyway, I'll give you my number too, in case you want to look at it again before deciding. It really is a nice place, and I know it might sound sentimental, but I really hope it ends up going to a nice person like you, Lilah."

Reid dropped her off half an hour later at her house. She was lost in thought, imagining how the store would look when it was set up the way that she wanted, and his voice jolted her back to reality.

"I'm glad you liked the store, Lilah. I thought it might be just what you were looking for. I think this cookie shop of yours is going to be wonderful," he told her, smiling. "Say, how are the cookies for the company party coming?"

"Um, great," she prevaricated. In truth, she hadn't done more than print off the recipes and make sure she had all of the ingredients for the three different types of cookies that she was planning on making. "I'm planning on doing some more work on them tomorrow morning." That part was true, at least. She didn't have to go in to work at the diner at all tomorrow, and she had already laid out the first recipe on the counter, spending a few minutes pouring over it before heading off to work that morning.

CHAPTER FOUR

T he next morning she got up, showered, and instead of changing into one of her usual outfits, put on clothes she wouldn't mind getting dirty: a loose shirt and a pair of old shorts. It got every bit as hot in her kitchen as it did in Margie's when she cooked, so without any air conditioning, shorts were a necessity.

She began by microwaving a substantial amount of butter until it was completely melted. With a slight twinge of guilt at how unhealthy these were going to be, she added in three tightly packed cups of brown sugar and half that amount of maple syrup. These definitely wouldn't be a good choice for anyone on a diet, but, well, who dieted around Thanksgiving, anyway? And everyone knew calories didn't count at holiday parties.

After the first three ingredients were combined into a gooey, sugary mess, she added the vanilla extract and eggs. The mix was really beginning to smell good. Lilah smiled as she imagined the people at Reid's work party biting into them and exclaiming over how good they were. If she managed to pull this off and make the hundreds of cookies for his event on her own, then it would just go to show that she *could* do this, despite the doubts that other people had about her... despite the doubts that she had about herself.

She mixed the dry ingredients next, then slowly added it to the bowl of melted butter, sugar, and syrup. After adding just a touch more flour to firm up the dough, she wrapped it in plastic and put it in the freezer. The waiting was the hard part; there was no way she could make the dough chill faster, so she'd have to wait at least an hour before putting the cookies in the oven.

"I guess this is the perfect time to clean," she said halfheartedly, looking around at the kitchen. It looked like a tornado had come through at some point. How had she managed to get flour on Oscar? "At least if I clean now, I'll be able to relax once the cookies are done."

Tidying up the kitchen wasn't as bad as she expected. After she turned on music and made herself a cup of coffee, it was almost fun. Still, she resolved to get better at cleaning up after herself as she cooked. Margie seemed to do it without thinking; her kitchen was almost always spotless when she finished whipping up a batch of something tasty.

By the time her kitchen was back to its pre-cookie state, it was time for her to preheat the oven and prepare the cookie sheets. She'd never even owned parchment paper prior to the beginning of her cookies adventures a few months ago, but now she had a few rolls stashed away in her pantry. It was amazing, really, how much more use she got out of her kitchen these days.

After lining the cookie sheets with the parchment paper, Lilah scooped out rounded spoonfuls of dough and laid them a couple of inches apart. Before she knew it, two trays were in the oven, and the other two were ready to go. One thing that she loved about cookies was how quickly they baked. In just a few minutes, her whole house smelled like maple syrup. The warm scent reminded her of Margie's kitchen. She glanced out the window, wishing that her friend could come over and taste one of the first cookies with her. She didn't begrudge the older woman her time with her family, but she did miss her.

A few minutes later, the oven beeped, signaling that the first batch of cookies was ready to come out. Lilah slid her hands into her new set of oven mitts—a gift that she had bought for herself after deciding to open the cookie shop—and pulled the trays out. She set them on racks to cool and put the second set of trays into the oven.

Too impatient to wait, she poured herself a glass of milk, pulled a small plate down from the cupboard, then took a spatula and carefully scooped up one of the still hot cookies from the tray.

She sat down at her small kitchen table and broke off a chunk of the cookie with her fingers. After blowing on it to make sure it was cool enough, she popped it into her mouth. Her eyes closed as she chewed blissfully. The test cookie tasted as wonderful as it smelled; it seemed to melt on her tongue, and had a strong but not overpowering, maple flavor. The maple brown sugar cookies instantly made it onto her mental list of favorite recipes.

Just as she was standing up to get a second cookie, her cellphone rang. She experienced a moment of mental panic, wondering if she had been scheduled to work after all and had somehow forgotten. When she saw that it was just Reid calling, she felt a rush of relief, tinged with a hint of annoyance. She was sure he was calling to check up on how the cookies were doing. If he didn't trust her, then why had he placed such a big order with her? With a sigh, she wiped a cookie crumb off her hand and answered the call.

"Hello?"

"Lilah," he said. "I'm afraid I have some bad news."

"What is it?" she asked, glancing toward the oven. Her annoyance from a moment ago was replaced by cold dread. Whatever this was, it couldn't be good. Was he going to cancel the order?

"Pete's dead," he said.

It took her a moment to understand what he had said. "Wait, Pete? The guy who showed us the shop? He's dead? What happened?"

"From what I've heard, suicide."

Silence fell between them. Lilah didn't know what to say. She could hardly grasp what *he* was saying. Suicide? Pete had looked tired when she'd seen him the day before, maybe a bit worn down, but *suicide*?

"That's terrible," she whispered.

"Yeah." Another moment of silence, then, "I just thought you should know. I'm not sure what's going to happen to his store now. It might be a while before things get figured out."

"Of course. I feel so bad for him." She sat down at the little kitchen table. "Thanks for calling me, Reid."

He ended the call and she put the phone down. She stared at it, stunned. Then she stood with a jolt; there was the distinctive smell of something burning, and smoke was rising from the oven. She must have forgotten to set the timer for the second batch of cookies. When she pulled the tray out of the oven, she was crushed to see the cookies burnt to a crisp.

CHAPTER FIVE

L ilah tossed the entire second batch of the maple brown sugar cookies in the trash, then turned her attention to the perfectly done first batch. They were cool enough now for her to remove them from the parchment paper and begin putting them in plastic containers, which she did. Once the containers were full, she secured the lids on them and stacked them neatly in the freezer. She would just have to make more cookies a different day to make up for the ones that she had burnt. She couldn't face the thought of pulling everything out to make another batch again. After the news she had just heard, she was likely to burn those cookies, too.

After she was done in the kitchen, she picked up her phone again, this time to call Margie. She had already told the older woman about how perfect Pete's store had been, and now had to be the bearer of bad news and tell her that it probably wasn't going to work out. Lilah had no idea who the store would go to now that Pete was gone. If he still owed money on it, it might go to the bank, she thought, but she didn't know what they would do with it. Like Reid had said, it would probably take a while to get everything straightened out.

Her neighbor was just as upset by the news as she was. She invited Lilah over immediately, offering to talk about the death of Pete.

"But what about your family?" Lilah asked.

"Oh, Robby's taken the kids out to the farm—they've cut down all the corn, but they're still offering hay rides and tours, you know. Eliza's here, but she has a headache and has been staying in the guest room all morning. As long as we're quiet, we shouldn't disturb her. You can help me with lunch, if you'd like. I'm just getting started on some homemade tomato soup. I figure soup and grilled cheese sandwiches will be just the thing to warm the kids up when they get back."

"If you're sure I won't be intruding…"

"Not at all, dear. I could use the company."

So Lilah changed out of her cooking clothes—she really needed to buy an apron, how had she forgotten the last time she was at the store?—and headed over to Margie's house after a saying a quick, affectionate goodbye to Winnie and Oscar. Her friend's kitchen was already full of mouthwatering scents when she walked in; not its usual warm vanilla, but onion and garlic and tomatoes. A pot was bubbling away on the stove, and a loaf of rye bread from the local bakery was sitting on the counter.

"What is this town coming to?" Margie asked with a shake of her head after greeting Lilah. "Two murders in as many months, and now a suicide. Vista used to be such a wonderful, family-friendly place. I'm not sure I even feel safe going out after dark alone anymore."

"Don't say that," Lilah said. "Vista's still wonderful. None of those deaths were connected. I'm sure every town goes through a rough patch every now and then."

"I know." Her friend sighed. "It's just that I knew Pete. Not well, of course, but my husband and I used to stop at his store every Sunday evening for a sandwich after our stroll in the park."

"The sandwich shop must have been open for a while," she said. Margie rarely talked about her husband, and Lilah didn't know anything about Mr. Hatch other than that he had died a few years before she'd moved to Vista.

"Oh, it's been there for years and years," Margie said. "Always in the Talbot family. I think Pete's father passed it down to him about a decade ago, though of course he's worked there much longer."

"Wow, so it must really have been a blow when he decided he had to sell it," Lilah said.

"I can't even imagine what that poor lad was going through. I'm sure he did everything in his power to keep the place."

Lilah, who had been wondering whether Pete's death was really a suicide or not, realized that it wasn't that far-fetched an idea. Faced with the prospect of selling the store that had been in his family for generations must have driven him to the end of his rope. With the fact that he was by the sound of it, deeply in debt, she could begin to see what might have caused him to do it. Still, it was hard to believe that the man she'd met only the day before, who had seemed so nice, had really ended his life shortly thereafter.

Continuing to gossip about Pete and the sandwich shop, she set to work helping Margie make lunch. She'd never made tomato soup herself before, so the casual cooking session quickly became a learning experience. The older woman seemed unable to turn down an opportunity to pass on her skills, and Lilah wasn't complaining. She had been spending a lot more time in the kitchen lately, but almost exclusively for cookie making. Since a diet of only cookies

47

didn't really appeal, no matter how good they tasted, she figured it wouldn't hurt to learn how to make some other dishes.

"The soup's done boiling," her friend said. "Could you get the food mill out of the cupboard by the stove? Run the soup through, then put it back on the burner on low to keep it warm. I'll start slicing the bread for the sandwiches."

"Sure." Lilah opened the cupboard and looked inside. "But ah, what does the food mill look like, exactly? I've never used one."

Margie bustled over and got it out for her. "Mine's a bit old-fashioned, I'm afraid. It's already set up. Just pour the soup in— slowly, so it doesn't splash, and turn the handle."

She did as she was told, and after only a couple of minutes found herself with a bowl of what very closely resembled the premade tomato soups that she had grown up on. Meanwhile, Margie had managed to carve the loaf of bread into slices of almost uniform thickness, and was busily buttering the bottom of a large pan.

"I'll make the kids' fresh when they get home. What would you like on yours?" she asked. "I've got American, cheddar, and swiss cheese, corned beef, fresh tomatoes… really anything you could want on a grilled cheese sandwich."

"Oh, you don't have to, Margie. I don't want to be a burden."

"It's no trouble at all, dear. What will it be?"

"Just swiss cheese and corned beef then, if you're sure." The truth was, she was hungry, not having eaten anything other than a cookie for lunch so far, and all of it sounded pretty good to her. Thinking of the cookie made her realize suddenly that she did have something to contribute to this meal, after all. Promising to be right back, she hurried of to her house to grab a container of cookies, promising herself that she would make up the difference next time she worked on Reid's order.

When she got back to Margie's house, Eliza was sitting at the counter with a blue ice mask pressed to her eyes. She looked up when Lilah came in, then replaced the mask over her face.

"It's these migraines," she was telling her mother-in-law. "They just make life miserable. It's hard enough, trying to have a career and also be a mother. To be saddled with debilitating pain once a month on top of everything else, well, it's a burden."

"My mom used to get migraines," Lilah said as she set the container of cookies down on the counter. "She tried every medicine under the sun, but nothing worked until she stopped drinking caffeinated beverages and began using essential oils around the house."

"I don't think giving up my morning coffee is going to solve this for me," Eliza said. "These are tied to my hormones. Every month, like clockwork." She sighed and laid her head down on the counter.

"Do you remember going to Talbot's Sandwiches last time you and Robby came to visit?" Margie asked as she flipped a sandwich over in the pan.

"That little place downtown that had insanely low prices?" the other woman mumbled, her eyes still hidden behind the mask. "I only remember because Robby told me his dad used to love that place."

"That's the one," Margie said. "Well, the owner committed suicide—"

"When?" Eliza asked, sitting up suddenly.

"I don't know," Margie said, sounding surprised. She looked to Lilah, who shook her head.

"I don't know exactly. It would have to have been either last night, or early this morning."

"Didn't you see him yesterday?" Eliza asked, peering at Lilah through a hole in the mask. "I remember her saying something about you buying the sandwich shop. My migraine was coming on then, so I wasn't listening closely."

"I did. I saw him yesterday afternoon."

"That's interesting," the other woman said, removing the mask and turning it over so the colder side would be pressed against her face.

"How so?" Lilah asked. The woman had a way of making her feel on edge.

"Well, it's going to be sold a lot cheaper if the bank auctions it off, isn't it?" Eliza shrugged and closed her eyes again. "It just seems like a useful coincidence for you. From what I heard, you were absolutely in love with the place."

"What are you saying?" Lilah asked, beginning to get angry. "Do you think I killed him?"

"I'm just saying it's a coincidence, that's all," the woman said. "You know what, Margie? I think I *will* take my sandwich and soup down to the guest room. Thanks."

With that, she got up and, still pressing the mask to her face, vanished through the doorway that lead to the dining room and the rest of Margie's house. Lilah was fuming. Eliza had only been here a few days. What right did she have to throw around accusations like that?

CHAPTER SIX

It seemed that Eliza hadn't been the only one to suspect Lilah's connection to Pete's death. The next morning, she got a call from the police station asking her to come in to answer some questions. Eldridge, the detective on the other end of the phone, didn't say what for and she didn't ask. She could guess. He already didn't like her, and had probably jumped at the opportunity to link her to something nefarious.

Annoyed at the situation, though still shocked enough by Pete's death not to complain, she called Randall at the diner and told him that she'd probably be at least an hour late. He told her it was fine, and when he heard the reason for her tardiness, said that he'd be interested to hear her recount her tale when she came in. The diner was a hot spot for gossip. She was sure her story would be spread around town by the time it closed that evening.

The Vista police station was a small standalone building on the edge of town. Lilah parked next to one of the two police cruisers and sat for a moment in her car, trying to figure out just why she felt so anxious. She hadn't done anything wrong, but there was still a bundle of nerves in her stomach. It likely had to do with the fact that her previous encounters with Detective Eldridge never exactly ended well. He thought that she was a nosy busybody, prone to interfering with police investigations. Was he likely to believe anything she said during this interview?

After mentally bracing herself, she walked through the front doors to see him waiting by the receptionist's desk. He waved her over without a word, and she followed him back to his office. She tried to convince herself that it was a good sign that he hadn't brought her to the interrogation room—maybe she wasn't a suspect after all.

"Ms. Fallon, can you tell me in detail about the last time you saw Pete Talbot?" he asked after gesturing for her to sit down in a chair across the desk from his comfortable leather seat.

She had been expecting this, of course. She had opened her mouth to tell the tale, when something occurred to her. How had Eldridge known about her meeting with Pete? She and Reid had been the only ones there… other than that scruffy drunk. She figured the chances of him knowing her name were pretty slim, though. Perhaps Pete had written their meeting down somewhere so he wouldn't forget it, or maybe Reid, who had been acquainted with Pete, had already been interviewed. Deciding it didn't really matter, Lilah cleared her head and got back to telling her story.

When she was done, Eldridge offered her a glass of water, then began asking her questions.

"What price was he asking for the store?" She told him. "Do you feel that was a fair price?"

"Yes," she said. "And well within my budget."

He held her gaze for a moment, then nodded and crossed something off the notepad in front of him. "What was your first impression of Pete when you met him?"

"He looked tired," she said, remembering the bags underneath his eyes.

"Anything else?"

"I don't know… he seemed nice. When we got there, he was arguing with a guy who said Pete owed him money?"

"What was this man's name?" Eldridge asked, showing a spark of interest for the first time.

"Andrew," she said. "I didn't catch his last name."

He nodded and made a note. "And you said 'we'? Who else was with you?"

"Reid Townsend came with me to see the shop," she told him. How did he know about her presence, but not Reid's?

He made another note, then asked her if there was anything else she wanted to tell him. When she said there wasn't, he stood up and led her out of the room. "We'll call you if we need anything else."

With that, she was free to go.

Lilah went straight to the diner, eager for the hours. When she walked into the kitchen, she almost ran over Kate Emery, her favorite of the other employees. The two women got along well, and had often mentioned meeting outside of work to get coffee or go shopping, but so far their schedules hadn't aligned.

"Oops, sorry," she said, catching the tray that Kate was carrying just as it began to tip.

"That was my fault," the other woman said, taking the tray back from her gratefully and straightening the dishes. "I didn't call out that I was coming through. I wasn't expecting you here this early."

"Talking to Eldridge didn't take long. Did Randall call you in to cover for me? Sorry you had to come in for such a short time"

"Yeah, but I'm glad you got here early. I've got an exam to study for today."

Kate was taking classes at the community college a few towns over with the dream of eventually becoming a nurse.

"Good luck on the test, I'm sure you'll do well," Lilah said, stepping back and holding the door for her co-worker.

"Thanks!" Kate said brightly as she walked past. "I'll just drop this order off, and pop back in to tell Randall I'm leaving."

Randall Price owned the little diner. He was an old man who seemed perpetually grumpy except to those who knew him well, and was rarely found outside of the kitchen during the hours the restaurant was open. The diner had one back-up cook, but Lilah didn't think he'd been in for months.

When he saw her come into the kitchen, he beckoned her over to where he was frying a hamburger patty on the grill and told her to spill the beans. Lilah wasn't surprised that he was interested in the suicide—it was an almost unheard of tragedy in Vista—but *was* surprised when she found out that he knew Pete Talbot.

"How did you know him?" she asked.

"I watched little Petey grow up," he said, flipping the patty with a satisfying sizzle. "His father, Samuel Talbot, was this diner's main competitor in town. He was also one of my best friends back in the day."

"He was your main competitor *and* your friend?"

Randall gave a rare smile. "We used to make bets on who would make more sales each month. When his wife got cancer, I donated a portion of the diner's profits to a fundraiser for her hospital fees. I never married, but I know he would have done the same for me." He shook his head. "Poor Pete. I'm sure glad Samuel isn't around to see this."

Lilah didn't know what to say in response, so she busied herself instead with putting on her apron and name tag. Randall was silent until she returned from taking the burger out to the guest at table three.

"When you saw Pete, did he say anything about his sister, by chance?" he asked as she returned and began to load up a plate with a double order of fries.

"I think he mentioned something about a sister, yeah," she said. "It was just in passing, though. Why?"

"Beth went away for college right after she graduated high school, and hasn't been back since." Randall said. "I've got an old letter that her father wrote to her before he died. It's sitting in my office right now, in fact. Look, if you hear from her about the sandwich shop, could you ask her to stop in? If I'm not here when she comes by, you can give her the letter yourself."

"Of course," Lilah promised. She grabbed a fresh squeeze bottle of ketchup from the counter and put it on the tray next to the fry order before bumping the swinging door to the dining area. She paused in the doorway and looked back, feeling an unusual surge of pity for the old man. She tried to imagine what it would be like to get the news that someone she knew, someone she had watched grow up, even, had killed themselves. She couldn't fathom it. It was bad enough when it happened to a near stranger.

Resolving to work extra hard around the diner in the coming days so Randall wouldn't have to worry about a thing, she let the door swing shut behind her and hurried over to the table of three impatient teenagers to deliver their fries.

CHAPTER SEVEN

L ilah had been so distracted by Pete's suicide that all thoughts of the Thanksgiving cookie order for Reid's company had been temporarily driven out of her mind. When she glanced at her calendar a couple of days later and saw the day of the event circled in red permanent marker, panic set in with a vengeance. She had less than a third of the cookies done. If another disaster happened, like when she had burned half of the maple brown sugar cookies, she would be hard pressed to make it up in time.

Deciding that if she was serious about this, she had to start acting like it, she made up her mind to reserve the entire afternoon for cookie baking. This time, she wouldn't let herself get distracted and burn half of them.

The maple brown sugar cookies had been an undeniable success, and she was confident that they would be a hit at the event. She was a little bit less certain about the next type of cookie she had planned; a spin on chocolate chip cookies, made with white chocolate and toffee instead of the usual semi-sweet chocolate chunks. She wasn't usually a fan of white chocolate, and wasn't sure whether her attempt at baking with it would be successful. That, combined with the fact that she had decided to make her own toffee instead of picking some up at the store, made her more nervous than usual.

The recipe for the toffee didn't *look* too difficult. The ingredients, at least, were simple; butter, sugar, salt, and vanilla extract. All she had to do was mix them together in a saucepan over medium heat, then pour the mixture onto a baking sheet lined with parchment paper to cool. She read through the recipe again, beginning to feel more confident. This shouldn't be that hard at all.

Making the toffee went smoothly for about ten minutes, until Winnie scratched at the door and whined to be let outside. Lilah gave the melted sugar and butter a quick stir, but the pan seemed to be taking a while to heat up, and she figured she'd be safe stepping away for a minute to let her dog outside.

When she got back, she found a congealed mess on the bottom of the pan. Disappointed, Lilah turned the burner off and brought the pan over to the garbage can before attempting to scrape the mess out. Despite her best efforts, a good portion of it remained stubbornly stuck to the bottom of the pan. Feeling like this was a sign that maybe she had bitten off more than she could chew, she filled the saucepan with warm water from the tap, squirted some dish soap into it, and put it in her sink to soak while she tried to tackle the toffee again.

This time, she stayed by the pan the entire time, stirring constantly until it was the right color. She shut off the burner, poured the mixture over the parchment paper, and put the tray in the fridge to cool.

When she checked on it again after scraping the last of the hardened sugar off of the first pot, it had solidified into a perfect tray of toffee. She broke off a small piece, popped it into her mouth and smiled. Despite her disastrous first attempt, it really hadn't been that hard. She had learned her lesson; when the directions said to stir something constantly, chances were they meant it.

It was time to get to work on the cookies. It was a nice, cool, breezy day, so she opened all of her windows and turned the radio up before pulling the now familiar cookie ingredients out of the cupboard. Flour, brown sugar, white sugar, shortening… at heart, all cookies were similar. This part, mixing together wet and dry ingredients, she could practically do with her eyes closed. The recipe was very similar to the one for normal chocolate chip cookies, except for white chocolate chips and crushed toffee.

Twelve minutes later, the first, perfect-looking batch of cookies came out of the oven. While they cooled on a rack, she put the next batch in and cleaned up the kitchen. With a little bit of trepidation, she settled down at the kitchen table with a still-warm cookie and a glass of milk. If she had done something wrong and messed up the recipe somehow, then she would be out hours of work and a lot of expensive ingredients.

She took a bite out of the cookie, chewed slowly for a moment, then grinned. The cookie wasn't bad at all. The homemade toffee made it work, she decided. Relieved, and feeling bolstered by her success, she finished her cookie, took the second batch out of the oven to cool, then went into the living room to see if there was anything good on the television.

She had only been relaxing for a few minutes before the sound of shouting made her sit up straighter and mute the made-for-TV drama that she had settled on. Looking toward her open window, she realized the sound was coming from Margie's house.

Concerned, Lilah stood up and walked over to the window, leaning on the sill and peering out through the screen. Her friend's window, directly across the yard from her, was open as well, and she could see her neighbor standing with her back to it.

"You've only known her two years, Margie, this is getting ridiculous!" The person shouting was out of sight, but Lilah was almost certain it was Eliza's voice.

"She's a good, true friend, and I don't want to hear anything else about it," Margie replied. She wasn't shouting, but her voice was loud enough that it carried easily across the yard.

"She's taking advantage of you. Not only of you, but of your children as well. What happens when she takes the money and vanishes, huh? Or even if she does open a cookie shop, what are you going to do when it inevitably fails, and she's not able to pay you back? Don't forget, that's Robby's inheritance that you're playing with."

"Robby has been nothing but supportive," Margie said. "Are you sure it's *his* inheritance you're worried about?"

This was the closest that Lilah had ever heard her friend come to losing her temper. She knew she was eavesdropping, but despite the guilt she felt at overhearing a conversation that she obviously wasn't meant to, she couldn't seem to stop.

"Just because he hasn't brought his concerns up with you, doesn't mean he doesn't have any," Eliza shot back. "How well do you really know this woman? Don't you think it's at all suspicious that she moved in to the house right next to you, and two years later she's asking you for money? I don't want to see you get taken advantage of, and *I'm* the bad person in all of this?"

"Eliza, I've told you already, she didn't ask me for a dime. I offered to help her. This cookie shop is something I've always wanted to do myself. But I've never had the time or the courage to take the plunge. I'm more than happy to help her do this, and I have complete faith that Lilah's going to be marvelous at running her own business."

At this, Lilah was finally able to pull herself away from the window and slide it shut. She was touched beyond words that her friend had so much faith in her, and it just made her feel all the worse for listening in. She didn't feel like she deserved the confidence that Margie seemed to have. When had she ever succeeded at anything in her life? Well, sure, she had gotten through college okay, and she hadn't messed up horribly when she was working for her father, though she hadn't enjoyed it. And she made an okay waitress. Other than that, well, she kept track of the years by her failures.

As much as she didn't want to admit it, Eliza had a good point. There was no risk of her taking the money and running, of course, but what if something happened that was beyond her control and she was unable to pay Margie back? She knew that it was extremely likely for a small business to fail. In fact, she had read somewhere that most small businesses failed in the first five years. The cookie shop was a gamble. Could she really take that risk with someone else's money?

Her phone rang, dragging her out of her thoughts. Pushing her doubts to the side, though she knew they would come back with a vengeance while she was lying in bed that night, she grabbed her cellphone from the coffee table. She felt a twinge of trepidation when she saw her mother's number on the screen.

"Hi, Mom," she said, throwing herself down on the couch.

"Lilah, it's good to hear your voice. How are you doing?"

"Good. How're you and dad?"

"Oh, fine." Her mother gave a tinkling laugh. "Busy as usual. I got your email, dear, and I thought we should talk in person."

Lilah sat up straighter at the words "in person." She had regretted sending her mother an email about her plans for a cookie shop almost immediately after it left her outbox.

"I thought your father and I could come down for dinner and discuss your plan together," her mother continued. "Are you free tomorrow night? I know it's short notice, but one of his meetings got canceled, and he doesn't know when he'll be free to make the trip again."

Her mind raced as she tried to think of an excuse good enough to get her out of dinner with her parents, but she couldn't come up with anything. "Yeah, I'm free," she said reluctantly.

"Wonderful," her mother said. "We'll pick you up at eight. You think of where you want to eat, all right?"

Lilah was in a daze as they said goodbye and hung up. She hadn't seen her parents for almost a year. Spending time with them, especially with her father, was always stressful. She knew that she was a failure in their eyes, and always felt bad about disappointing them. She couldn't imagine her father would have anything good to say about the cookie shop. Why, oh why, had she sent her mother that email?

She sighed and rested her head against the plush cushions of the couch. There was one good thing about the fact that they were going to come to town on such short notice; at least she wouldn't have long to dread their visit.

PATTI BENNING

CHAPTER EIGHT

T asked with finding a nice place to eat dinner that evening, Lilah took advantage of the slow morning at the diner to read reviews of nearby restaurants on her phone. Vista was a small town, and wasn't exactly crowded with places to eat. There was the diner, of course, a few fast food places scattered along Main Street, a pub, and an Asian restaurant that served everything from sweet-and-sour chicken, to Indian food, to sushi. None of them were what her parents would consider "nice," so she widened her search to include nearby towns.

She finally found a place that looked promising. It was called the Vintage Grill, and seemed to have a wide enough variety of food to please all three of them, and the pictures on the website showed a nice, upscale restaurant.

When she got out of work, Lilah texted her mother the address, then turned her attention to her wardrobe. She hadn't exactly had much of a reason to keep her closet stocked with the sorts of clothes that her parents would like. She had a few dresses that might have worked if it had been summer, but they wouldn't fit with her mother's sense of fall fashion.

"Well, I guess I need a new outfit for Thanksgiving, anyway," she said to herself as she shut the closet door. "I might as well head into town and see what I can find."

There was a nice consignment shop in town where she did most of her clothes shopping. She had found some unique items there over the past few years, and she loved how much variety they had compared to normal retail shops. She never knew what she was going to find when she walked in, but she was almost always pleasantly surprised.

Today was no exception. Just minutes after walking in, the perfect dress caught her eyes. It was dark blue, and fit her perfectly when she tried it on. It fell to her knees, and flared out when she spun in place for fun. Lilah smiled; there was no way her mother would be able to find anything to criticize about this simple, yet elegant dress.

Just in case her parents wanted to pop into her house before going to the restaurant, she also picked up some potpourri, good toilet paper, and a new light bulb for the fixture above the bathroom mirror for good measure.

When she got home, she spent a little bit of time tidying up, and pulled some of the cookies out of the freezer for good measure. If she had more time, she would have loved to bake fresh cookies for the smell, but at least the potpourri would make her kitchen smell like something other than the onion rings that she had heated up for lunch.

By the time she started getting dressed for dinner, her house was spotless and smelled strongly of cinnamon and nutmeg. Winnie and Oscar had both had nail trims, she had straightened up the pile of shoes in her front closet into something that almost looked organized, and she had pulled her nicest glasses to the front of the cupboard. The little yellow house didn't look too bad at all, at least as far as she was concerned. It almost looked like she was doing well for herself.

She put on the blue dress, then spent a few minutes fiddling with her hair. Eventually she decided to just leave it down, but curled it for good measure. She dug the charm bracelet that her mother had given her years ago out of a drawer and put on the diamond necklace that her father had given her after her first promotion while she was working for him. Her relationship with her parents had been strained, to say the least, after she had very publicly quit her job at her father's company. She felt no shame in wearing their gifts in a suck-up attempt. She had no idea how this dinner would go, or how they would respond to her plan to open the cookie shop, and she didn't think it could hurt to do what she could to tweak the odds in her favor.

Despite her misgivings, she met her parents at the door with a smile, and invited them inside. She hugged her mother, whom she had always been closer to, and after a moment's awkwardness shook her father's hand.

"I forgot what this place looked like," her mother said, peering around the kitchen. "It's cozy. I wish you'd have me over more, dear. I know your father's busy a lot, but I'm only an hour away and I'd be happy to drive down here for the weekend sometime."

"I know, Mom, I've just been so busy lately," Lilah said. It was even true; she'd spent almost a month working two jobs, and only rarely had time free.

"You're so like your father," her mother said with a sigh. "Anyway, where is your bathroom?"

Lilah gave her directions, then turned to face her father. He was a dignified looking man in his late sixties. His hair was steel grey, and his build strong despite his age. He had always been so busy with work that they'd never really had time to bond when she was a child, and she had always found him slightly intimidating. That hadn't changed. Right now, he was looking at her with his brow creased in a frown. Not a good sign.

"Do you want a cookie?" she asked, gesturing to the small plate of maple brown sugar and white chocolate toffee cookies that she had brought out.

"Maybe after dinner," he said, not glancing at them. "You know how your mother feels about having dessert first."

Neither of them said anything after that. The tension in the room lessened only slightly when Lilah's mother reappeared and announced that she was ready to go.

The Vintage Grill was everything that Lilah had hoped when she chose it, and then some. She was relieved that at least one thing was going right this evening. Certainly, her father would be more inclined to forgive her for whatever she had done to earn his displeasure this time over some good, hearty, southern-style food.

She and her mother made small talk while they waited for the waitress to bring them their drink orders. Lilah was just beginning to think that the evening would go better than she expected, when her father cleared his throat and put his menu down.

"When your mother showed me that email you sent her, I was very concerned," he said. "You aren't serious about this cookie business, are you?"

"Well, yes, I am," she said. "But there's no need for you to be concerned. I'm not asking you for money—"

"That's one of my concerns, Lilah. You told your mother you're borrowing the funds from a friend. That's a recipe for disaster, and I hope you know that. Have you considered what would happen if you have a disagreement? What if she wants more control over the company than you're willing to give her?" He shook his head. "You would have been better off coming to us for a loan, or better yet, come work for me again if you're so eager to jump back into the business world that you, quote, 'hate with a passion'."

"I've already apologized for saying that, Dad," she said. She was disappointed, but not surprised. Ever since she had quit her job at his company, he had thrown her parting words back into her face every chance that he got. "I don't think it's fair to compare opening a small store to sell cookies with a high-stress corporate job."

"It may seem different to you, but they're in the same world. The same principles apply. It's business, Lilah. It's not going to be a walk in the park."

"I'm not expecting it to be," she said. "Why are you so upset? I thought you'd be glad that your daughter was finally doing something serious with her life."

"I don't consider opening a cookie store in a tiny town that isn't even a dot on the map to be 'doing something' with your life," he said, the frown line between his brows returning even deeper than before. "You have never had realistic expectations. Look at how you bounced from job to job after you left the company. Do you know how many times your mom's told me that you'd found your new career path, only to hear from you again a few weeks later when you were back working as a waitress in that grease trap? This won't be any different."

"It *will* be different —"

He cut her off. "You're right, there is a difference. This time, you're wasting someone else's time and money, not just your own."

Lilah didn't have a reply to that. He had touched right upon the heart of her concerns, and she knew that he was right. It was reckless and selfish of her to risk Margie's money on the cookie shop.

"Look," he said with a sigh, "if you want to get back into the business world, I'd be happy to hire you back into the company. You can start at the same salary you were at before, and I'd be surprised if you didn't get a promotion within a year. We can forget about these last few years. I'd be willing to consider them a sort of mid-life crisis on your part."

"I don't want to work for you again," Lilah said, her tone more hollow than argumentative. "I'm sorry, Dad. I wish you approved of this, but I'm going to do it with or without your blessing."

CHAPTER NINE

L ilah's mood was dark for the rest of the evening. She sent her mother, who was refusing to take sides in this renewed schism between father and daughter, home with a container of cookies, and bid them both an icy goodbye in her driveway. Then she retired inside, prepared to watch television for the rest of the evening, with Winnie curled up next to her, Oscar on the chair across the room, and a mug of warm cider in one hand and cookie in the other.

Despite her best efforts at spoiling herself, her mood didn't improve any until she got a call from Reid. He told her the first bit of good news that she'd heard all day.

"I just heard about another building that's going to go up for sale," he told her. "Since we don't know what the deal is with the sandwich shop yet, well, I thought you might want to take a look."

"I do," she said, sitting up straighter. "Where is it?"

"On Crest Drive," he told her, naming a side street in town. "So the location isn't as ideal as Pete's place, but it doesn't look like a bad little shop from the outside. On the plus side, the guy who's selling it contracts out to the machine shop. I'm sure he'll give you a good deal, especially if I go to look at it with you."

"When are you free?" she asked, eager for anything that would distract her from the disastrous dinner with her parents.

"I could do tomorrow morning," he said. "Are you working the morning shift at the diner?"

"Hold on..." She hurried into the kitchen to double-check the schedule on her fridge. "Nope, evening. Tomorrow morning's perfect. What's the address? I'll meet you there."

He gave her the address and then bid her goodnight. Lilah realized that it was getting late, and decided that she ought to head to bed as well. First, she pulled out her laptop and searched for the address that Reid had given her. It belonged to a small concrete laying business. The building was cute, with a red awning out front, but she wasn't sure it screamed "cookie shop." Still, it wouldn't hurt to check it out. At the very least, it would take her mind off of everything that had happened this evening.

The next morning, she left early and got to the little shop before he did. She waited in the car, gazing at the building. It was small, but so was the sandwich shop. This building stood alone on its own lot, instead of sharing space with its neighbors, which she supposed should have been a plus, but she had liked the way Pete's place had been nestled between the two other stores.

"But this place is available," she told herself. "And no one knows what's happening to Pete's. I've got to start being more realistic." Her father's comments had stung, but she knew that they had at least a kernel of truth. If she wanted to have any chance of success in starting her own business, she had to be realistic.

There were some things that she liked about the building. The red awning, for one, and the flower bed in front. It had its own parking lot, which she was sure would come in handy. She resolved to reserve her final judgment until after she had seen the interior.

When Reid finally got there, she got out of her car and met him at the building's front door. "So why is the guy who owns this building selling it?" she asked.

"He's expanding, and doesn't use this location as much anymore," he told her. "He called me while I was driving. He had to run out to pick something up for his daughter, but he told me he left the door unlocked, and we're welcome to go in and take a look around before he gets back."

Lilah pulled open the door and walked into the empty building ahead of Reid. The first thing she noticed was that it was dark; there weren't many windows, and the ones that were there were small. It didn't have anything like the nice, big display window that she had loved so much at Pete's sandwich shop.

She flicked on the lights, and wasn't impressed with what she saw. The building looked comfortable enough, but it didn't look like the sort of place where one would sell cookies. The floors were carpeted, and the layout was cramped. There were a few small rooms, and one tiny kitchen in the back. If she owned it, she could knock down some of the walls, but that would be a lot of work and expense on top of the cost of the building.

The truth was, the sandwich shop had been perfect. Even though she tried not to, it was impossible not to compare the two. She knew her dad would tell her to be realistic—she couldn't expect to have a wide variety of storefronts to choose from in such a small town, after all—but she couldn't ignore her gut, which was telling her very clearly that this was not the place for her.

"I hope he gets here soon," Reid said, glancing at his watch.

"If you have to go somewhere, I can just call him about the building," Lilah told him. She appreciated him taking the time out of his day to meet her out here, and didn't know how to tell him that she had already decided that this wasn't the place for her.

"I'm supposed to stop in at the police station before noon," he told her. "Detective Eldridge wanted to talk to me."

"About Pete's suicide?" she asked, knowing that she was probably being nosy.

"That's just it," Reid said with a frown. "I'm not so sure it was suicide."

"What do you mean?" she asked, looking up at him sharply.

"Well, you saw that other man that was there when we met him at the sandwich shop," Reid said. "It turns out that Pete owed him a lot of money. A *lot* of money. He had some sort of gambling problem. One of our mutual friends, a guy named Jackson, stopped in to see me at my office to talk about business, and the subject of Pete came up. He'd heard about Pete's death, but didn't know it was suicide. He asked me if I knew who had killed him. When I told him that Pete had taken his own life, he acted surprised. Apparently, Pete had called him only hours before his death and they had made plans for another big-stakes poker game."

"That doesn't mean he didn't kill himself," Lilah said. "Maybe he realized that he was about to lose even more money by gambling on the poker game. He could have gotten overwhelmed and decided to end it."

"According to Jackson, Pete regularly won a lot of money at poker. Between the game and selling the store, he should have been able to pay off most of his debts."

Lilah frowned. If Reid was right, then maybe Pete *hadn't* killed himself. Did that mean there had been another murder in Vista?

"Do you think that guy, Andrew, we saw when we got to the store could have done it?" she asked.

"I've got no idea, but I'll mention him to Eldridge. I'm going to tell him what Jackson told me. If this was a murder, then Pete deserves some justice."

CHAPTER TEN

After Reid left for the police station, Lilah called the person that owned the building and told him thanks for letting her look at it, but that she didn't think it would suit her needs. She was a bit disappointed, but mostly she couldn't stop thinking about what Reid had said. What if Pete had been murdered? It wouldn't change anything about the availability of his store, of course, but somehow it made a world of difference to how she felt. When she'd heard of his suicide, her predominant emotion, after shock, had been sorrow. The thought of murder, however, made her angry. Even though he'd had his issues, Pete had seemed like a nice guy. He definitely hadn't deserved to have his life brutally ended by some drunk that he owed money to.

Lilah drove back home, distracted by thoughts about Pete and the unfairness of the world. She stopped to get gasoline on the way, taking her time picking out a bottled iced tea inside before filling up at the pump. It wasn't until she was nearly to her house that she glanced at the clock and realized that she had fifteen minutes until her shift at the diner was supposed to begin.

She left her car running and dashed into her house to let Winnie outside and change into a different set of clothes for work. After letting the dog back in, she swiped the list for the last set of cookie ingredients that she needed from the counter and ran out the door. She got to work just as the second hand on the clock in the diner swept past the twelve.

"Lilah?" Kate said, sounding surprised when she pushed her way into the kitchen. "What are you doing here?"

"Sorry I'm late," Lilah gasped. "I had a busy morning… saw Reid… talked about murder…"

Kate blinked. "You aren't late. Didn't Randall call you? He changed the schedule yesterday because I needed to switch around some of my hours. You didn't need to come in until two."

"Oh. Which number did he call? I didn't get anything on my cell…"

They both looked around to Randall, who was just dumping a new batch of potatoes into the fryer.

"He probably called your home phone," Kate said apologetically. "You know how he is about cellphones."

"It's all right," Lilah told her. "I can just head back home for the next two hours. It's not like I live far away. Or maybe I'll stick around and get lunch here. I'm in the mood for something chock full of flavor and calories."

"Well, you've come to the right place," Kate said with a smile.

Lilah fetched herself a cup of soda and put an order for a double cheeseburger with the works with Randall, then settled into a corner booth and pulled out her phone. She wanted to talk about Pete's death with someone, but she didn't know who she could reach out to. Reid, of course, was busy, and besides, he had known the man personally. It didn't seem right to try to talk about it with him. Margie had her family over, and the last thing that she wanted was for Eliza to hear her gossiping about a dead man. Suddenly it hit her. Of course: Val. She didn't know why she hadn't thought of her best friend sooner. Granted, the two of them hadn't been seeing each other as much lately due to the fact that Val's fiancé had recently returned from a business trip overseas. Lilah decided to send her a text to see if she was free to swing by the diner—her boutique wasn't far—and have lunch with her.

"I got your message just in time," Val said as she slid into the seat across from Lilah. "I was just about to go out and get Chinese for lunch, but of course this is nicer. Sorry I haven't been stopping by as much lately."

"It's fine," Lilah assured her. "How's Joel?"

"He's glad to be back," Val said. "And it's good to have him back."

"I bet. He was gone a while this time."

"It should be his last big trip before the wedding."

Val and Joel had been engaged for almost six years, and had been dating each other for much longer than that. Somehow the date for their wedding kept getting pushed back. Lilah was relatively sure that it would happen this time, but then she'd thought the same thing the year before when it got canceled due to Val's father ending up in the hospital after a heart attack. The two had met in high school, and as far as Lilah knew had been together ever since.

"You two are lucky to have each other," she said, thinking of her own dismal love life.

"You'll find someone like Joel too, one day," her friend told her. "I'm sure of it. Besides, maybe it's good that you don't have any romantic distractions right now. You've got more important things to focus on."

Lilah knew Val was talking about her cookie shop. She sighed and picked at the huge pile of fried beside her burger. "Do you think I'm doing the right thing?"

"Are you having second thoughts?" Val asked.

"Well, my parents came to town last night…"

"Oh, don't listen to them," her friend said, stealing one of her fries. "Your dad's still sore about you leaving the company. He wouldn't be happy even if you became the president of the United States."

"I just don't understand why he *cares* so much," Lilah said, all of the old bitterness coming back. "I'm his daughter. Isn't he supposed to want me to be happy? If I had children, I'd tell them to follow their hearts. I wouldn't be angry at them if they did something differently than what I had planned out for them."

"He's, what, seventy?" Val asked.

"Almost."

"My guess is, he's getting worried about what's going to happen to his company when he's gone. He probably wants to keep it in the family."

Lilah couldn't help but think of Talbot's Sandwiches. From what Margie and Randall had said, the sandwich shop had been handed down for generations, always staying in the same family. Was that what her father wanted? Was she being selfish by following her own dreams?

"I don't know," she said slowly, thinking back over their conversation the evening before. "He doesn't seem to think I'm responsible or realistic enough to run my own business. I don't see why he'd want me in charge of his."

"I've been telling you since you moved here, the two of you need to sit down and talk without arguing sometime. Neither of you are very good at communicating in emotional situations like that."

"Well, next time I see him, I'll invite you along to mediate," Lilah promised. "I don't know, I guess one of the reasons that dinner last night upset me so much was because I know that a lot of what he said was right. I keep messing things up. I haven't kept a job, other than working here, since I left the company. What makes me think that I can run my own business? The thought of failing at this terrifies me. So much is at stake, and it feels so different than all of the other jobs I've tried."

"Well, there you go," Val said. "With everything else you've started, you always seemed to jump in feet first, without a care in the world. I can tell already; you're acting differently with this whole cookie shop thing. You're being more careful, taking your time. You're going to be fine, Lilah."

"But what if I'm not? Even if I do everything perfectly, the store could still fail. I should never have accepted Margie's loan. It's not fair of me to put her savings on the line too. I—"

"Whoa," Val said, putting a hand on her arm. "Calm down. Margie's a grown woman. She knows what she's doing, okay? If she wasn't prepared to take risks, she wouldn't have offered you the money. I don't like hearing you doubt yourself like this. You're usually so confident. What's gotten into you?"

"I don't know. Maybe it's just because of what Eliza said," she said with a sigh. Seeing Val's blank look, she added, "Margie's daughter-in-law," and proceeded to tell her friend about her interactions with the other woman over the past week.

When she was done, her friend snorted and said, "Well, it sounds to me like this Eliza is more worried about how much money she's going to inherit from Margie than anything else. Some people get ugly when it comes to money."

Val's comment brought Lilah full circle to the reason why she had wanted to talk to someone in the first place; Pete's death. A thought popped into her mind, but she quickly dismissed it. Eliza might not be the most pleasant person in the world, but there was no way she would have committed murder just to keep Lilah from getting the storefront that she wanted. Instead, she told Val about Reid's theory that Pete had been killed by the drunk man he owed money to.

She and her friend spent the next twenty minutes discussing reasons that people might have had to kill Pete, and by the time they were done, Lilah was convinced that his death had indeed been a murder and not a suicide. It just didn't make sense to think that someone on the verge of pulling himself out of debt would choose to end it all just weeks before he could finally pay off the money he owed.

CHAPTER ELEVEN

L ilah woke up the next morning with a twisting stomach and sweaty palms. It was the day before Reid's party, and she still had dozens of cookies to make. That fact alone wasn't what was making her so nervous that she felt sick, though. This event would be her first real test as a professional baker. If people liked the cookies and nothing went dreadfully wrong, then it would be great publicity for her cookie shop, but if the cookies weren't a hit or she somehow messed up the order, her new career could be over before it began. She was grateful toward Reid for taking this chance on her, but right now a part of her was wishing that she had never even heard of his company party.

After work the evening before she had stopped at the little grocery store in town for some last-minute shopping. She had saved today's cookies for last for two reasons: one, they would be the most difficult, and she hadn't wanted to risk getting discouraged before completing the two simpler recipes; and two, she didn't think they would store as well in the freezer as the maple brown sugar and white chocolate toffee cookies had.

Lilah dragged herself out of bed and walked into the kitchen to see the pile of apples waiting for her just where she had left them on the counter the night before. She stared at them for a long moment, wondering what she had gotten herself into. There was no way she could make all of the caramel apple pie cookies she needed to in time for the party tomorrow. What was she thinking, choosing such complicated cookies? She should have played it safe and done something simple, but it was too late now. She had all of the ingredients, and the recipe was printed. She would just have to do the best she could.

The recipe was in four parts, and she started with the dough first. It was different than regular cookie dough, more like pie crust, but luckily it was pretty straightforward; in no time at all, she had four balls of dough wrapped in plastic wrap in the fridge to chill.

Beginning to feel more confident—that part had gone easily enough, after all—she turned her attention to the next section; the caramel. As she read through the instructions, she realized that the process was similar to how she had made the toffee a few days ago, with a few differences such as the addition of heavy cream. She managed to melt the sugar and stir in the other ingredients without burning anything, which she considered to be a great success.

The caramel made, she turned her attention to peeling and slicing the apples, which was boring, but not difficult, and didn't have much potential for error, then mixed the apple pieces with sugar, cinnamon, nutmeg, and a dash of lemon juice to keep the apples from turning brown.

Her anxiety from that morning had all but faded by the time she had finished with the apples and put them in the fridge. With ample time while the dough chilled, she decided to take a shower and get cleaned up. The messy part of baking, mixing all of the ingredients together, was done. Actually assembling all of the cookies would be much more time consuming, but at least she wouldn't come out of it covered in flour.

After she was dressed, she felt more like herself. She called Reid and confirmed the details for the party the next evening. She was supposed to arrive at six to drop off and arrange the cookies. He had asked her if she would be able to stay for the event, but she had politely declined. Even though she had seen a lot more of Reid lately, and was slowly beginning to realize that maybe he wasn't quite the work-obsessed clone of her father that she had originally thought, she was still reluctant to do anything that might mislead him about her interest in a relationship. Like Val had said, she had more important things to worry about right now.

After she got off the phone with Reid, she decided that it was time to tackle the rest of the project and finish the cookies. With such a unique recipe, she figured it would be a good idea to make a small batch first. That way, if anything needed to be tweaked, she wouldn't have wasted all of those ingredients.

Lilah grabbed one of the balls of dough out of the fridge, unwrapped it, and placed in on a cutting board that she had sprinkled with flour. She began tackling the dough with the nice marble rolling pin that she had bought during her shopping trip the previous night, occasionally dusting the top of the dough with flour to prevent it from sticking. After some trial and error, she had a reasonably thin slab of dough rolled out on the cutting board. She put the rolling pin to the side and pulled a drinking glass out of the cupboard. The one thing she had forgotten to buy was a cookie cutter, but this should work just as well.

She cut two circles of dough and used a spatula to transfer them from the cutting board to a parchment paper covered cookie sheet. Careful not to spill any, she took a small spoonful of the apple pie filling and placed it on top of one of the dough circles, then added a dollop of the homemade caramel on top. She covered the entire thing with the second circle of dough, crimped the edges with a fork, carefully slit the top with a knife, then put the single cookie into the preheated oven to see how it turned out.

The caramel apple pie cookie was not a disappointment. She ate it gingerly just as it came out of the oven, and burnt the roof of her mouth on the filling in the process. It was well worth it. The cookie was easily better than any full-sized apple pie she had ever had. It would take her a while to make the rest of the cookies for Reid's work event, but she no longer regretted choosing the recipe. Who could resist these bite-sized apple pies? She had a feeling they would be the party favorites. The other two kinds of cookies were good, but were nowhere near as unique as these.

It was late afternoon by the time she finished baking the rest of the cookies. It was a wonderful feeling to drizzle homemade caramel on the very last cookie and know that for better or for worse, she was done. Whatever happened the next night, she knew that she had made her best effort, and she was proud of every single one of her cookies.

After tidying up the kitchen and putting the cookies up and out of reach of Winnie, she was beginning to feel a little bit stir crazy. She had been cooped up in her house all day. What she really needed, she decided, was some fresh air. It had been far too long since she'd gone on a nice long jog through town. Now that she had her car back and in working order, she hardly walked anywhere.

It felt good to get back in her running shoes and exercise pants. She did a few stretches in her house before leaving through the front door and setting off at a slow pace down the road. Before she managed to find her rhythm, she was halted by the sound of her name. Margie had come out of her house and was waving her down. Lilah noticed that the minivan was absent from the driveway; her family must have gone somewhere without her.

"I was just about to go over to your house and see if you needed any help preparing for tomorrow," her friend said when Lilah met her on the walkway up to her house.

"Actually, I just finished with the last of them," she told the older woman. "Thanks for the offer, though. How's everything going for you?" She wondered if Margie would make mention of her argument with Eliza, but her friend just smiled and told her things were going very well.

"Now, I thought we ought to talk about the schedule on Thanksgiving. I know we had dinner late in the evening last year, but this year I was thinking we would do it a bit earlier in the day, since the children are here," Margie said. "Do you think two o'clock would work on your end?"

Lilah gazed at her friend in surprise. She hadn't been expecting to be invited to Thanksgiving dinner this year not with the older woman's family in residence. She had vaguely planned to crash

Val's party, but had been too focused on getting through her first big cookie order to give it much thought. "You want me to come over this year?"

"Yes, of course," Margie said. "Though if you have plans with your own family…"

"I definitely don't," Lilah said, thinking back to the terrible dinner with her parents a few nights before. "I'd love to come, if you're sure everyone else is okay with it."

"They'll love to have you," her friend said with a smile. Lilah thought that might be an exaggeration, but she didn't push it.

"What do you want me to bring?" she asked instead.

"Oh, just bring yourself. Come over a little early, and you can help me cook if you'd like. I've got the meal all planned already. I'm going to do the last of the shopping today."

"I'll come over in the morning and help you put everything together," Lilah promised her friend. "Thanks, Margie. I can't wait."

She meant it. Even though the older woman's daughter-in-law disliked her, she thought she would enjoy having a big family Thanksgiving for once.

CHAPTER TWELVE

L ilah began preparing for Reid's work event as soon as she got home from work the next afternoon. Her car wasn't exactly designed to carry such a large load of cookies, but she made do with some creative stacking and very careful driving.

Reid met her at a side entrance to the office building where the event was being held, adjacent to the machine shop. He was wearing a black dress shirt with the top button undone, and looked undeniably attractive. Lilah felt suddenly grungy in her boot cut jeans and pink blouse. She had dressed down on purpose in hopes that he would get the message and not ask her to stay; besides the fact that she wanted to keep her relationship with Reid purely professional at this point, she wasn't exactly inclined to spend the evening with a bunch of stuffy business types. Still, she almost regretted her decision to turn down his invitation when she saw what waited for them inside.

"Wow," she said. "You guys really go all out for Thanksgiving, huh?"

Reid smiled. "This is our annual employee appreciation dinner. It's a nice way to kick off the long Thanksgiving weekend. There's food, drinks, a raffle, and an award ceremony. It really isn't like the boring work events you're probably thinking of."

She looked down, not wanting to admit that she had expected it to be exactly that. "Where do the cookies go?" she asked, changing the subject.

"On that table over there." He gestured to an empty table on the other side of the room. "Some of the office ladies said they were going to pay for a cake together, so we should probably leave some space on one side of the table for that. I'd like about half of the cookies set up on platters. The other half can go in the other room for now; I'll have someone put them in little bags for people to bring home if they want."

With his help, Lilah carried the cookies in and arranged them on platters on the table. When they were done, she took a step back and gazed down at their work. The cookies looked just like something a professional catering service would have provided.

"Let me know how it goes," she said, grabbing the empty containers that she had brought the cookies in.

"Are you sure you don't want to stay?" he asked.

"I'm not really dressed for it," she pointed out. "Besides, tomorrow's Thanksgiving, and I'm helping Margie cook. I'd better rest well tonight, or I won't be able to keep up with her."

He laughed. "All right, I suppose you've got a point. Thanks for all of this. The cookies look wonderful, and I'm sure people will enjoy them."

"Thanks for being my first customer," she told him. With a wave, she backed out the door and headed for her car. "I'll see you later."

With the stress of the big cookie order over and done with, Lilah felt like a different person. For the first time, it hit her that Thanksgiving was tomorrow, and just a month after that, Christmas would be there. Then came the new year and with it, a whole new future for her... if she ever found a suitable place for her cookie shop, that was.

Instead of going home, she decided to drive by Talbot's Sandwiches. Maybe there would be something posted on the door about it still being for sale. With any luck, the bank would decide to auction it off. She still held out some hope that she would be able to buy it. Despite the fact that its previous owner had died a violent death, she still felt a fondness for the store. Pete, she was sure, would want his family store to end up in good hands.

There was no sign on the door when she drove by. Instead, she saw something surprising; there were lights on inside.

"Who in the world could that be?" she muttered as she eased her car around the corner. It didn't take her long to park and walk back around to the front of the building. She peered in through the display window, but the front room was empty. She was debating on if she should knock, or whether it would be rude to interrupt whoever was inside when she heard raised voices coming from inside.

She hesitated for only a moment before pushing the front door open. One of the voices was a woman's and the other sounded like a very angry man.

"I know he's dead. I still need the money he owes me. C'mon, Beth, I got your brother out of a tight spot. You need to do the same for me."

"No, you need to leave, Andrew. I'm not discussing this with you."

Lilah gasped. Andrew. The same man she and Reid had seen when they came to look at the sandwich shop. And Beth... why did that name sound so familiar?

"I am not leaving!" Andrew shouted. "I'm not taking no for an answer. You get me that money, or else—"

"Or else what? You're going to call the police? Everyone knows you saw him just hours before he died. Do you really want to draw more attention to yourself?" Beth snapped. "My brother's gambling problem is not my concern. You're going to have to take a loss on this just like everyone else does."

There was the sound of footsteps. Lilah just had time to duck back outside before a woman with mouse-colored hair and a pinched face appeared. Trailing behind her was the same man Lilah had seen with Reid. He looked sober now, but his face was flushed with anger. Beth yanked open the door. Her gaze flitted over Lilah before she looked back over her shoulder to Andrew.

"Leave, Drew. Now."

With a huff, the man left, brushing past Lilah on the way out as if she wasn't there. He smelled strongly of stale cigarette smoke, and she recoiled reflexively.

"The sandwich shop's closed," Beth said. She began to shut the door.

"Wait. Are you Pete's sister?" Lilah asked. She was beginning to remember her conversation with Randall the week before. She was certain that was where she had heard the name Beth before.

"Yeah," the woman said, eying her cautiously. "Did he owe you money?"

"No, nothing like that. Actually, I was interested in buying the store from him. My name's Lilah Fallon. I saw Pete the same day he died."

"Really?" Beth gave her a curious look. She hesitated for a moment, then opened the door wider. "Do you want to come in?"

Lilah followed her back to the kitchen, where the woman had a pot of coffee waiting. There was a mess of papers and manila file folders on the counter.

"I've been trying to figure out the financial mess my brother left behind," Beth told her. "I knew my dad made him a mistake when he left him the store."

"He seemed to really care about the sandwich shop, from what I saw," Lilah said.

The other woman shrugged. "If you say so. So, you saw him the day that he committed suicide? What was he like?"

"Well, I don't know. I mean, it was the first time I'd ever met him..."

"Did he say anything odd?"

"No," Lilah said. "Not that I remember." She hesitated. "Beth? I don't want to over step any lines here, but how well do you know Andrew?"

"Drew? Pete and I went to high school with him. He's always been a little bit… out there… but he seems worse than ever now. Why?"

"It's just that, from what I heard, your brother was on the verge of being able to pay off his debts. A friend of mine mentioned that it doesn't make sense for someone who's about to be debt free, someone who's been working toward getting his life on track, to kill himself just hours after making arrangements to sell his restaurant. I can't even imagine what you're going through right now, but I know if it was my family, I'd want to know if there was even the slightest chance that their death wasn't quite what it appeared to be."

"Are you saying you think my brother was murdered?" Beth asked. "And you think Andrew did it?"

"I don't know," Lilah said, "but after what I just saw, well, Andrew definitely seems like the sort of guy who could lose his temper. Sorry, I probably shouldn't have brought any of this up."

"No, it's fine," Beth said, turning her coffee mug slowly in her hands. "Andrew does have a short temper, and he's not exactly reasonable. Have you spoken to the police about this?"

"A friend of mine—he knew Pete, too—went to the police after he found out more about how close Pete was to being able to pay off his debts. I haven't spoken to them since the day after his murder."

"He told them about Andrew?"

"I think so," Lilah said.

"Good." Beth said. "I'll be sure to keep away from him if he comes around again. Thanks, Lilah."

"No problem. I just don't want anyone else to get hurt."

"You're a good person." The other woman gave her a tired smile. "What was it that you came by for? I think you mentioned something about buying this place before we got off topic."

"Yeah, Pete gave me a tour that day and I fell in love with this place."

"What sort of business do you have?"

"I'm opening a cookie shop," Lilah told her. "It's all still in the beginning stages."

"Hmm." Beth glanced toward the messy pile of papers, her brows drawing together as she thought. "If you're still interested in it, would you consider a lease instead?"

"A lease? For how long?" she asked, her heart beginning to beat faster. Was she going to be able to use this building for her cookie shop after all?

"I'd have to think more, but a few years at least. I don't want this store to leave the family for good, but right now things are so bad that I'm not sure I'm going to be able to keep it open. It's no wonder Pete kept blowing me off when I wanted to meet him to talk about the store; he was probably embarrassed. He's been buying supplies on credit for months, and I don't have the cash sitting around to pay it all off before the collection agencies start coming around. If I could lease this place out for a couple of years and save up enough money to get out of the financial hole that Pete dug himself into, then I might be able to reopen and run the sandwich shop myself eventually... debt free."

"So I'd lease this place for a couple of years, then I'd have to find somewhere new for the cookie shop to move to?" Lilah asked. It wasn't exactly what she had been hoping for... but it just might be better than nothing.

Beth nodded. "I'm sure you'll want a larger store front after a couple of years anyway."

"I'll think about it," Lilah said. "There are some people I have to talk to first. Is it all right if I have someone else come and take a look at this place?"

"That's fine. Would you be able to come out tomorrow?"

"Tomorrow's Thanksgiving."

"Oh, shoot. I completely forgot," Beth said. She rubbed her temples. "With everything that's been going on, I hadn't realized… If a different day works better, that's fine. But I need to figure out what I'm going to do about money as soon as possible."

"I understand," Lilah said. "I'll talk to my friend and see how soon we can get out here."

The two women exchanged phone numbers and bid each other goodbye. Lilah looked back at the sandwich shop as she walked out. She did love the place. Maybe she could figure out a way to make the lease work. At least it would be less money and less risk if things went wrong. She was glad that she had decided to drive past the little restaurant that evening. Talking to Beth had been a stroke of unexpected luck. Now all she had to do was see if Margie fell in love with the sandwich shop the same way she had.

CHAPTER THIRTEEN

Margie's kitchen smelled like cranberry sauce and stuffing when Lilah walked through the front door to her friend's house the next morning. The kids were running amok, and Lilah had to dodge two of them on her way over to the sink to wash her hands. Eliza, thank goodness, was nowhere to be seen.

"Happy Thanksgiving," Margie said. "There are some cinnamon rolls on the counter over there. Help yourself, but don't wreck your appetite for dinner."

"Thanks, these look great," Lilah said. "So, where should I start?"

"Could you do the mashed potatoes? I've got to finish the pies."

"Sure."

With her, Margie, and the three kids coming and going out of the kitchen, the warm room was unusually crowded. It was a big difference from the way her friend's house usually was—quiet and peaceful. Somehow, though, all of the activity just added to the festive feeling of the day.

Lilah set to work peeling the potatoes without complaint, keeping an eye on the older woman as she prepared two perfect-looking pies to go into the oven. The pumpkin pie reminded her of the very first cookies that she had helped Margie bake—pumpkin spice cookie cups—and the apple pie made her think of the cookies she had made for Reid's event. She had gotten a text from him late the night before, telling her that the cookies had been a hit and thanking her again, but she wanted to know more. Which cookies had people liked the best? Had anyone asked him who made them? It was too bad she hadn't thought of the perfect name for the cookie shop yet, because it would have been a great way to advertise her business without spending a dime.

She put the potatoes in the water to boil, then leaned back against the counter and glanced at the clock. An hour and a half until they were supposed to start eating. She was tempted to take another cinnamon roll because her stomach was growling, but at the same time she wanted to be hungry for the meal. Nothing was better than sitting down at a full Thanksgiving spread with an empty stomach. She was fully prepared to eat her weight in turkey today.

Deciding to distract herself from her hunger, Lilah began telling Margie about her encounter with Beth the day before. Her friend listened as she worked. Her face remained unreadable until Lilah finished her story.

"What do you think?" she asked. "Is it better to lease the perfect building for a couple of years, or buy a building that isn't as good, but at least would be ours?"

"How long a lease did she decide to offer you?" Margie asked. "If it's just a two-year lease, it probably isn't going to be worth the time and effort it would take to relocate to another location. But if it's, say, five years, that might be more realistic."

There was that word again. Realistic. Was she really so bad at being realistic?

"I don't know," she said. "She told me she'd have to think about it. I guess Pete left the sandwich shop in a lot of debt that she wasn't expecting, and she needs to pay it off before she can get it up and running again."

Suddenly she remembered Randall telling her that he had a letter to Beth from her deceased father. How could she have forgotten that? She made a mental note to tell Beth as soon as possible.

"If it's for five or more years and you think it's a good idea, then I don't see anything wrong with accepting her offer of a lease," Margie said. She bustled over to the oven and pulled it open to stick a meat thermometer into the turkey.

"It might be a better idea than buying," Lilah said, picking up her train of thought from the previous evening. "It would be less money up front, for one, and if the cookie shop fails, well, it's probably easier to get out of a lease than it is to sell a storefront in a tiny town like this."

"I'm happy to support whatever decision you make," her friend told her with a smile. "Here, can you set the stuffing on the counter? I need room on the stove to begin sautéeing the green beans."

Lilah obliged, setting the huge pot of homemade stuffing on the counter next to the paper towel roll. It smelled amazing. She had always been a fan of stuffing, and as she had discovered last year, Margie made the best stuffing around.

She turned her back on the pot, telling herself that she didn't have too much longer to wait before eating. She was just reaching for a fork to test the boiling potatoes when she heard a loud crash behind her. Both she and Margie jumped. Lilah looked around with horror to see that the pot of stuffing had fallen and spilled across the floor. Jacob, Margie's grandson, was standing next to it with a strip of paper towel in his hand and a stricken look on his face.

118

"I'm so sorry," he said. "I didn't mean to, Lexi told me to get paper towels because she spilled something and my elbow bumped it and it fell…"

"It's all right, dear," Margie said, recovering much more quickly than Lilah. "You go give your sister the paper towels, then come back here to help me clean up."

"I shouldn't have put it so close to the edge," Lilah said, staring sadly at the spilled stuffing.

"This isn't anyone's fault," her friend said firmly. "Accidents happen."

"Do you have the ingredients to make more?"

"No, I used up everything in that batch." The older woman heaved a sigh. "I'll have to see if someone can go out and get some pre-made stuffing mix."

"I can do it," Lilah said. Despite her friend's kind words, she felt that a large portion of the blame should rest on her own shoulders. She should have made more room elsewhere on the counter, and not set the pot on the edge right by the paper towels.

"Are you sure? You know what, I'll send Eliza with you. You two should get to know each other better, and besides, she mentioned that she wanted to pick up a bottle of wine and some sparkling juice for the kids before the meal. I'm sure she won't mind going out."

Lilah winced. The idea of spending even a short amount of time alone in the car with a woman who so clearly disliked and mistrusted her wasn't appealing, but she was reluctant to tell Margie how she felt about her daughter-in-law. Besides, it was her fault the first batch of stuffing had been ruined. She wasn't about to make even more trouble for the woman who had been so kind to her.

"All right," she told Margie. "I'll go wash up and grab my car. Write down whatever you think you'll need, and I'll be happy to go and pick it up."

PATTI BENNING

CHAPTER FOURTEEN

E liza climbed into Lilah's car in icy silence. Neither of them was happy with this arrangement, but it was hard to say no to Margie when she wanted something, especially when the older woman always made so many sacrifices for everyone else. Lilah had no doubt in her mind that her friend fully knew that the two women would rather be anywhere but in the same car together. This was Reid all over again; Margie was determined to throw the two of them together until they got over their differences and started to like each other.

While she had to admit that she was beginning to see Reid's more positive attributes, Lilah seriously doubted that it would be as easy to change her mind about Eliza, simply because the woman was not inclined to like her. At least Eliza seemed to agree with her about one thing: the less talking there was on this trip, the better. She didn't say a word as Lilah pulled out of the driveway. It wasn't until they had turned toward town that either spoke.

"Do you mind if I stop somewhere really quickly?" Lilah asked. They were about to pass the diner, and she had suddenly remembered Randall's note. She wanted to be able to give it to Beth the next time she saw her.

"Whatever you want," Eliza murmured, gazing out the window.

She turned the steering wheel a bit too sharply and pulled into the diner's parking lot. It was closed for the holiday and wouldn't reopen until Saturday, but Lilah had a key. Randall had mentioned that the letter was in his office. She hoped it would be easy to find. It seemed important to her that Beth get it as soon as possible. Thanksgiving was a holiday that was all about family, and she could imagine how much it would mean to the other woman to read her father's final words to her at last.

"Do you want to come in? I'm not sure how long this will take," she said. Eliza hesitated, then nodded. There was a curious glint in her eye that Lilah didn't like. Did the woman think she was going to steal something?

She unlocked the diner's front door and the two of them walked inside. The ovens had been off all day, but the restaurant still smelled like fried food. It was odd to be in there without Randall—

he was as much a fixture in the diner as the booths or the deep fryer. She wondered for the first time what her boss got up to during the holidays. He wasn't married and had no children as far as she knew. It was sad to think of him all alone at home during a time when everyone else was with their families.

"I need to get something out of the owner's office," she told Eliza. "It's through the kitchen." She realized that to an outsider, this probably seemed pretty shady. Still, she knew she wasn't doing anything wrong. She didn't like how Eliza's suspicious gaze made her feel like everything she did was criminal.

The kitchen was dark and silent. It was unsettling to see the restaurant so dead. Lilah flicked the lights on, then opened the door to Randall's small office, which wasn't locked. Eliza peered in after her, not bothering to hide her curiosity.

"What are you looking for?" she asked.

"Do you remember that man who died last week? He owned the sandwich shop that I was interested in buying."

Eliza nodded.

"Well, my boss here at the diner knew his family pretty well. The guy, Pete, has a sister named Beth who has been estranged from them since she left for college. Apparently, her father wrote her a letter on his deathbed and gave it to Randall to pass on to her if she ever came back. I'm looking for that letter now, because I might see her later today if Margie has the time to go with me, and I think she should be able to read her father's last words without having to wait any longer."

"Oh." The other woman blinked. It was obviously not at all what she had been expecting. "That's really nice of you."

Lilah shrugged. "I just know that if I were in her shoes, I'd want the letter." She thought of her own strained relationship with her father and felt a wave of guilt. Maybe it was time to put their old disagreements to rest at last.

She didn't like going through Randall's things, but he *had* told her she could give Beth the letter if he wasn't there. She thought that it would take a long time to search through all of the piles of paper in the office, but she found the letter right inside the second drawer she opened. It was in a yellowed envelope addressed to Beth in a shaky script. It was still sealed, the contents having been untouched for years.

"I've got it," she told Eliza as she slid the letter into her purse. "Let's —"

"Shh," the other woman hissed, raising her hand to Lilah off. "I thought I just heard the door open."

"The diner door?" Lilah whispered. "Are you sure?"

"Well I heard something. A bell jingled."

"That must have been it," Lilah said, her heart beginning to beat faster. The diner was closed for the day. No one should be here. Why hadn't she thought to lock the door behind them when they came in? "I'm going to go see what's going on."

She tiptoed over to the swinging door that led from the kitchen to the dining area and pushed it open just the tiniest bit. She pressed her eye to the crack. What she saw made her palms go sweaty. With infinite care, she eased the swinging door shut and turned to Eliza, her eyes wide.

"It's Andrew," she whispered. She realized that wouldn't mean much to the other woman. "He might have had something to do with Pete's death," she added.

"What is he doing here?" Eliza hissed back.

"I don't know. He drinks a lot, from what I've heard. He's also maybe a little bit messed up in the head."

"So what do we do? Sneak out the back?"

"I can't just leave a crazy guy in here on his own," Lilah said. "What if he robbed the place, or tried to make his own fries and burned it down?"

"Then what?"

"I don't know!" Lilah thought quickly. "Get your cellphone out and dial nine-one-one, but don't place the call yet. I'm going to go tell him we're closed and ask him to leave. If he does anything crazy, call the police."

It wasn't a perfect plan, but it was the best that either of them had at the moment. Lilah waited until Eliza had the emergency number ready to call, then she pushed open the door and walked out of the kitchen. Andrew, who had been staring blankly at the cash register, looked up when she came out of the kitchen.

"Hi, uh, I'll have a swiss mushroom burger with two patties, some onion rings, and a large diet soda," he said. His eyes were bloodshot, and she had the feeling he had been drinking again.

"Sorry, but we're closed," she told him, trying to sound as professional as possible.

"Closed?" he blinked at her.

"Yes, we're closed," she said firmly. "It's Thanksgiving."

"It is?" He ran his hand through hair that didn't look as if it had been washed in a week. "I just want a burger. Can you make me one anyway? I'll pay extra?"

"I'm sorry, but no. You have to leave now or we're going to call the police." She gestured to Eliza, who held up her cellphone. "They'll be here in just a few minutes if you try anything."

The mention of the police seemed to wake him up. He raised his hands and took a step backwards.

"Don't call the cops, all right? I didn't know you were closed. If they catch me drunk in public, they're going to throw me in the drunk tank again. I was brought in just last week; I can't afford to go again. No one's gonna pay my bail this time. C'mon, lady, don't call them. Please?"

"If you leave now, we won't," she told him.

He took a step toward the door, then paused and squinted at her. "Hey, didn't I run into you outside of Talbot's last week? I remember, 'cause the police picked me up two blocks away saying some lady had called me in for public intoxication. That was you, wasn't it?"

"You did run into me outside of Talbot's Sandwiches," Lilah admitted reluctantly. "But I didn't call the police on you."

"Musta been someone else, then," he said. "I'm goin', I'm goin'."

"Wait," Lilah said. Something occurred to her. "You went to jail that evening? The same night that Pete died?"

He nodded. "Yeah. Lucky that I did, I guess. The police thought I did him in, until I pointed out that I'd been snoozing off my buzz behind bars that entire night."

With that, he left in a hurry, apparently still concerned that she was going to call the police on him. Lilah gazed after him. If he had been in police custody the night that Pete died, then he couldn't have killed him. Which meant that his death probably *had* been a suicide. There would never be any justice for poor Pete.

CHAPTER FIFTEEN

Eliza's attitude toward Lilah seemed to improve greatly after that. She no longer sat in stony silence in the passenger seat, but talked animatedly about what they had just been through.

"Do you think he really didn't know it was Thanksgiving?" she asked. "Or was he lying to try to get us to not call the police?"

"I think he was probably honestly confused," Lilah said. "He didn't act violent or anything. I shouldn't have left the door unlocked when we went inside. With my car in the parking lot, he probably didn't think twice about walking in."

"Poor guy. It seems like a crappy way to spend Thanksgiving, walking around town drunk like that."

"Yeah," Lilah said, looking over at Eliza in surprise. "It does sound pretty miserable."

Margie's daughter-in-law seemed like a different person now that she wasn't glaring at her in suspicion. Maybe they had just gotten off on the wrong foot. After all, Eliza had just been acting out of concern for the older woman. Maybe Lilah just had to prove to her that she wasn't a bad person.

"Where to now?" the other woman asked.

"If you don't mind, I'd like to swing by the sandwich shop on the off chance that Beth is there," Lilah said. "It's on the way to the gas station to the south of town, which is the only convenience-type store that's going to be open today. I'm sure they have some boxes of cheap stuffing mix. Of course, it won't be nearly as good as Margie's."

"That's fine with me. The instant stuff only takes like five minutes to cook, anyway, so it's not like we're in a big hurry. And I'd kind of like to see the store that you and Margie have been talking so much about."

Lilah pulled into the parking lot behind the sandwich shop a few minutes later. She wasn't sure what Beth's car looked like, but there was a tan station wagon parked right behind the sandwich shop, so *someone* must be there. She and Eliza walked around to the front

PATTI BENNING

and knocked on the door. Sure enough, Pete's sister appeared a second later. She looked surprised but pleased to see Lilah.

"Come on in," she said, pushing the door open. "I just got here and started cleaning. I was expecting you to call before coming, but this is fine if you don't mind a little mess. Is this your business partner?"

"No, this is actually her daughter-in-law, Eliza," Lilah said. "I'm sorry that we just dropped by like this. We were on our way to the store, and I thought it wouldn't hurt to see if you were here. I've got something for you."

She pulled the letter out of her purse and handed it to the other woman, who took it with a confused look.

"What is this?"

"It's a note from your father," Lilah told her. "He wrote it before he passed away and gave it to my boss—who was his friend—before he died. It's for you."

Beth's eyes went wide. She looked from the letter to Lilah and back again. "From my father?" she repeated in a tremulous voice. "Thank you so much. Come on in, take a look around…" she said, trailing off vaguely as she walked back toward the kitchen. "I'll be with you in a few minutes."

She vanished into the tiny office. Lilah didn't blame her for wanting privacy to read the letter from her estranged father, though now she and Eliza wouldn't be able to leave until she came back out without being rude. The two women exchanged a look and Eliza shrugged.

"You might as well show me around," she said.

Beth reappeared just as Lilah got done giving the other woman the grand tour. Her face was streaked with tears, and she clutched the letter in her hand. Eliza wandered away to look at something on the other side of the kitchen while Lilah and Beth spoke.

"I think you two should leave now," Beth said. "I'm sorry, it's just this letter… it showed me what a mistake I've made. I need some time alone."

"I completely understand," Lilah said. "We'll get go—"

"Lilah, come look at this," Eliza interrupted sharply from near the sandwich shop's back door.

Shooting Beth an apologetic look, Lilah hurried over. She followed Eliza's gaze. The other woman was staring at a notice taped to the door. *Building to be auctioned 12/15 at 3:00 pm. Open for walk through 12/10 and 12/12.*

"What does that mean?" Lilah asked. "I don't understand."

"This store's going to be auctioned off," Eliza hissed. "Look, the bank owns it. She doesn't. She was lying to you, Lilah. I bet she was going to steal whatever money you put down for the lease and get out of town."

Lilah was shocked. The notice must be a mistake. She turned back toward Beth, her mouth already forming the words of the question that she was going to ask her, when she saw the small gun in the woman's hand. Fresh tears were rolling down her face.

"Just go," she sobbed. "Leave me alone."

"I don't understand," Lilah said. "The sandwich shop isn't yours?"

The tearful woman shook her head angrily. "It was supposed to be mine. I'm his only family, it should have gone to me when he died… but he took out a second mortgage on the place without telling anyone. The bank took the restaurant, and everything else that should have gone to me. Pete died for nothing."

"What do you mean he died for nothing?" Her eyes were on Beth's gun. It was small, tiny enough to easily fit into her purse. She seemed to have forgotten that she was holding it.

"Do you know I offered to buy the sandwich shop from him?" Beth asked. "He kept telling me that I didn't want it, that it was more trouble than it was worth. I thought he was just trying to get back at me for running out on the family after my dad gave him the shop. I didn't realize that he was trying to protect me from the mess he made. If only he had met with me, if he had talked to me like I had wanted, he could have explained everything. I'm so sorry, Pete. You drove me to it. Why couldn't you just tell me the truth?"

Beth shouted the last few sentences angrily. Lilah flinched as Beth waved the gun around, as if threatening Pete's ghost. She still didn't understand why the woman was having a breakdown in the middle of the sandwich shop's kitchen. Had the stress of the last few weeks made her snap?

A noise from behind her made her turn. Eliza was fiddling with the lock on the employee door, trying to undo it. Her face was pale and her hands were shaking. She looked up and met Lilah's gaze.

"She killed him," she gasped. "Don't you understand? She wanted the store so she killed him. We have to get out of here before she comes to her senses and realizes what she's said."

"That can't be true," Lilah said, horrified. "He was her brother, she couldn't have —"

The sound of a hammer being pulled back made her freeze. She turned slowly to look at Beth, who was pointing the gun, not at them, but at herself.

"I can't live with this," she said. "I can't. Please, just leave. Leave me alone. I'm going to rejoin my family."

"Wait," Lilah said. "Don't do this." Even if Beth was a killer, she didn't think she could bear to witness something like this.

"How can I live with myself?" the other woman asked in a hollow voice. "This letter... if only I had gotten it before I killed him. I would have realized that they never meant to hurt me. I was the selfish one. All along, it was me." She crumpled up the letter with one hand and tossed it toward the garbage bin. It bounced off and rolled toward Lilah's feet.

"Killing yourself won't solve anything," Lilah said. She was terrified, not for herself, but for the woman holding the gun. If what she was saying was true, then it was the letter that Lilah had delivered that had driven her over the edge. If she died, then that would make Lilah responsible for her death. She heard the sound of a lock clicking behind her, then the door opened and she heard footsteps receding. Eliza had left.

"Staying alive won't solve anything. It won't erase what I've done."

"Your father loved you, didn't he?" Lilah asked, glancing toward the letter at her feet. "Do you think he'd want both of his children to die? His final act was to write this letter to you. If you kill yourself now, after reading that letter, *because* of that letter, how do you think that would make him feel?" She faintly heard breaking glass from behind her, but had no idea what it could be.

To her relief, Beth lowered the gun slowly, a fraction of an inch at a time. Lilah stepped forward slowly, prepared to duck if the other woman showed any sign of turning on her. She reached for the gun and carefully slid it out of Beth's limp grip, then slid it across the floor away from them.

"Thank you," the woman whispered. "Thank you for stopping me from being selfish again. You're right, I shouldn't take the easy way out this time. I deserve to suffer for what I did to Pete."

"Please… just… sit down," Lilah said. She was shaking. She had stopped someone from ending her life, but it didn't feel quite as good as she had expected. The woman had killed her own brother because of greed, and had been fully prepared to take advantage of Lilah and steal her and Margie's money. Still, she didn't regret getting the gun away from her.

A minute later, she heard vehicles pulling into the parking lot behind the sandwich shop and before she knew it police were swarming through the employee entrance. Detective Eldridge put Beth in handcuffs, and another officer bagged the handgun. One of the men's shoes kicked the crumpled-up letter closer to her, and without thinking she bent down and picked it up. Smoothing it out, she read,

My dearest daughter,

I know we've had out differences over the years. You've always been a strong-headed child, and even though I never said it, I admired your stubbornness. You have deserved this apology for a long time, but my own pride made me put it off until now, when it's almost too late. My dear Beth, I am sorry for giving the sandwich shop to Pete instead of you. I didn't do it out of favoritism, as I know you believe, but because I thought Pete needed more help than you did. You have always made your own way in life, and I knew you would go far even without my help, but Pete's options were more limited.

I should have explained all of this to you the day of our fight. I should have known how important our family's restaurant was to you. I should have listened when Pete told me that he thought you should have it, that he wasn't interested in inheriting it. I thought you had put him up to it, but he tells me now that you never even knew that he had tried to get me to leave the sandwich shop to you instead.

It's too late for us to make up in this lifetime. I've made my peace with that, and I hope you know that I have always loved you. Please go easy on Pete. I know the two of you haven't always gotten along, but he's been a good big brother to you in his own way. He loves you and I love you, and I hope that one day you'll come back and put things right with what's left of your family.

Love,

Dad

Tears pricking her own eyes as she imagined what Beth must have felt while reading this, Lilah folded up the letter and handed it to one of the officers. She hoped it would find its way back to Beth eventually. It was saddening to think that the Talbot family had been torn apart because of one unsent letter.

PATTI BENNING

CHAPTER SIXTEEN

Thanksgiving was a day late at the Hatch household that year. After Beth's arrest, Lilah and Eliza had spent hours at the police station telling their part in the whole affair. By the time they were released and were able to return to Margie's house, the children were asleep and no one had the energy to bring all of the food out of the fridge. They had never gotten the stuffing, either. Margie made Lilah promise to come over at noon the next day, which she was more than happy to do.

She didn't get much sleep that night, lying in bed for hours, staring at the ceiling, and thinking of Beth and the Talbot family. She couldn't help but draw parallels to her own family; she didn't have any siblings, but her relationship with her father was just as bad. She didn't want to wait until her dad was on his deathbed to fix things between them. Despite their differences, they were still family. She didn't want to lose that.

Lilah still felt groggy when she went over to Margie's house the next morning. The table was still set from the previous day, and her friend was busily heating up the food that they hadn't been able to eat. Eliza was sitting at the breakfast bar, and gave Lilah a welcoming smile when she came in. This, more than anything, made her feel better. Being accepted by Margie's family meant the world to her.

"We had pizza last night because you got arrested," Jacob said brightly, appearing in the kitchen doorway. He was holding a foam sword, and was grinning at her as if she was the coolest thing he had ever seen. "Thanks!"

"She didn't get arrested, Jake," Eliza called after him as he dashed back into the living room. She shook her head. "Sorry. He was already asleep when I got back, and heard the story secondhand from Lexi."

"It's all right," Lilah said, laughing. "At least he's talking to me now. He seemed so shy the first time I came over."

"He just takes a while to warm up to strangers," Eliza said. "So do I, I guess." She looked embarrassed. "I'm sorry for the way I treated you before. I know it's no excuse, but I was worried you were going to take advantage of Margie. I've told her before that she's too trusting for her own good."

"It's fine," Lilah said. "I hope you know that I'd never do anything to hurt her. I feel bad enough about accepting the loan as it is."

"I know. Yesterday proved to me that you're a genuinely good person." She hesitated. "Speaking of yesterday, I've also got to apologize for breaking your car window. I panicked, and all I could think was that I needed to get to my phone, but the car was locked and you had the keys. I'll pay to get it repaired."

"Don't worry about it. I'm glad you called the police and they got there when they did. I don't know what I would have done if Beth had gone for the gun again."

"I'm glad you saved her," Eliza said. "I know she killed her brother, but I still don't like the thought of her dying. At least this way she'll get the punishment she deserves, and maybe she'll find a way to make peace with herself eventually."

"It's time to eat," Margie called from the dining room. "Sit down, everybody. Don't let it get cold."

Lilah took her place at the table. The food looked amazing, even after being reheated. There still wasn't any stuffing, but it didn't matter. It wasn't the food that made Thanksgiving, anyway.

"A toast," Margie said raising her glass. "To family."

"To family," Lilah repeated, clinking her glass with Eliza's. It was a simple toast, but it was perfect. This was what Thanksgiving was about: family, and friends, and being grateful for what they had. The food was just a bonus.

Made in the USA
Monee, IL
30 January 2022

90174150R00085